Fool's Mate

Shane Reed

Copyright

Copyright © 2024 by Shane Reed

All rights reserved.

Chapter 1

The golden sun cast a warm glow through the living room window, bathing the framed photographs in an almost ethereal light. Debbie sat on her cream-colored couch, her finger tracing the outline of her late husband's face in one of their wedding photos. His laughter seemed frozen in time, a cruel reminder that it had been six months since she last shared that joy.

"Michael, I miss you so much," she whispered, wiping away a tear that threatened to fall. An ache swelled in her chest, a mixture of grief and loneliness that she couldn't quite shake off. The emptiness echoed through the room, amplifying the weight of her solitude.

Hesitant to wallow any longer, Debbie took a deep breath and reached for her laptop. The weight of loneliness and longing for companionship had been pressing on her heart for too long, and she knew that she couldn't let herself be consumed by the void left after her husband's passing. As she sat in front of the screen, a mix of emotions churned within her—uncertainty, hope, and a tinge of apprehension. With a tentative click, she found herself on the homepage of an online dating website, the digital gateway to a world of possibilities and connections. It was a decision made out of both curiosity and desperation, a yearning to fill the void in her life and to once again experience the warmth of companionship. The cursor hovered over the "Create Account" button, her mind racing with questions and doubts. What if this was a mistake? What if she was opening herself up to more heartache and disappointment? But amidst the uncertainty, a glimmer of hope sparked within her, nudging her to take this step toward a new chapter in her life. She couldn't deny the longing for love and human connection, and she refused to let fear hold her back. With a determined exhale, she clicked the button, ready to embark on a journey of rediscovery and, perhaps, find a new source of joy and fulfillment.

"Alright, Michael, let's see if there's anyone out there who can make me smile again," she muttered to herself, the sound of her own voice echoing in the quiet room. It was a phrase she had repeated countless times, more out of habit and a sliver of hope than any real expectation. Her fingers danced across the keyboard, navigating through the profiles on the online dating website, each click accompanied by a mix of trepidation and a faint glimmer of anticipation. Her eyes scanned the screen, not quite knowing what she was searching for amidst the sea of faces and profiles. But then, amid the multitude of hopeful smiles and carefully crafted introductions, one profile caught her attention – Ryan Anderson. The name sent a jolt of conflicting emotions through her, stirring memories of a past she had tried so hard to put behind her. She hesitated, her cursor hovering over his profile, a whirlwind of thoughts and emotions swirling within her. Part of her wanted to click away, to avoid the potential pain of revisiting the past. Another part, however, was drawn to the familiarity of the name, the possibility of closure, or perhaps even a chance to confront the source of her past anguish. With a mixture of curiosity and caution, she clicked on his profile, uncertain of what she would find but willing to explore the unexpected twist of fate that had led her to this moment.

His charming smile radiated warmth, a stark contrast to the cold ache that had settled in Debbie's heart. She couldn't help but feel drawn to the genuine expression in his piercing blue eyes, and with a mix of curiosity and cautious optimism, she clicked on his profile. As she delved further into the details of his life, she found herself captivated by the intricacies of his personality. His love for hiking spoke to her adventurous spirit, while his passion for jazz music resonated with her own appreciation for soulful melodies. Reading about his dedication to volunteering at local animal shelters tugged at her heartstrings, evoking a sense of compassion and empathy within her. However, it was his unwavering commitment to supporting cancer charities that truly struck a chord with her. The cause was deeply personal to her, having lost

Michael to the relentless grip of the disease. As she immersed herself in the words on the screen, she felt a glimmer of hope and connection, as if the universe had orchestrated this serendipitous encounter to bring a ray of light into her world once more.

"Ryan Anderson... Can you really be as sincere as you seem?" she thought, her finger hovering over the mouse. The doubt lingered in her mind as she hesitated, wondering if this could be the start of something truly meaningful. With a deep breath and a quiet prayer, she initiated a conversation with him, her heart filled with a mixture of anticipation and apprehension. She longed for a fresh start, a chance to connect with someone who could understand her in a way that others hadn't. As the cursor blinked on the screen, she couldn't help but wonder if this was the moment that would change everything.

The soft glow of Debbie's laptop illuminated her face as she sat in the dimly lit room, the only source of light emanating from the screen as she carefully typed out her first message to Ryan. Her heart raced with a mixture of excitement and trepidation, the familiar weight of her wedding ring feeling heavier on her finger as she grappled with conflicting emotions. The gentle hum of the laptop filled the silence, creating an atmosphere of introspection and uncertainty as she contemplated the significance of reaching out to someone new. Each keystroke felt like a step into the unknown, a departure from the familiar routine of her life, and she couldn't help but wonder if this digital interaction would lead to a profound shift in her world.

"Hi Ryan, I'm Debbie. I was touched by your passion for supporting cancer charities. My late husband battled cancer, and it's a cause that's very close to my heart. It's nice to meet someone who shares that concern."

She hesitated for a moment before clicking "send," taking a deep breath to steady herself. The response came faster than she expected, with Ryan's words appearing on the screen in front of her.

"Hi Debbie! Thank you for reaching out. I'm so sorry to hear about your husband. Cancer is a cruel disease, and I've always believed that we need to

do everything we can to support those affected by it. By the way, I noticed in your profile that you enjoy hiking and jazz music too – I'd love to hear more about your favorite trails and artists!"

Debbie couldn't help but smile as she read his message. She felt an instant connection with Ryan, finding solace in their shared interests and his apparent empathy. They exchanged messages well into the night, discussing their favorite hikes, jazz musicians, and even sharing stories about their experiences volunteering at animal shelters. With each exchanged word, the trust between them grew.

"Maybe this is it," Debbie thought, her heart swelling with hope as she pondered the possibility of a new beginning. She found herself considering the prospect of rediscovering happiness, a notion that had felt distant and elusive for so long. As she gazed at the screen, her mind wandered through the labyrinth of her emotions, entertaining the idea that this virtual exchange with Ryan could be the catalyst for a transformative chapter in her life. The notion of happiness, once a distant dream, now seemed within reach, and she couldn't shake the feeling that this simple act of reaching out had the potential to reshape her future in ways she had never imagined.

***

The following weeks unfolded in a whirlwind of exchanged messages, intimate video chats, and late-night phone calls that seemed to stretch on for hours, as Debbie and Ryan delved into the depths of their lives. Their conversations traversed a myriad of topics, from the intricacies of their families and childhood memories to the fervent exploration of their most profound dreams and deepest fears. It was as if they had effortlessly bypassed the formalities of getting to know each other and instead plunged headfirst into the uncharted territory of genuine connection. Each interaction felt like a revelation, as they uncovered uncanny similarities and shared experiences that seemed to weave their lives together in a way that defied the mere passage of weeks. The bond they forged transcended time, creating the illusion that they had known each other for years, rather than the brief span of just a few weeks.

Debbie found herself smiling more frequently, the corners of her mouth naturally curving upwards, and laughter flowed from her lips with an ease that had eluded her for months. She marveled at the transformation within herself, recognizing that Ryan's presence in her life was the catalyst behind this newfound joy. His empathetic nature and genuine understanding had a remarkable effect on her, casting a warm light on her recent struggles and illuminating the path towards healing. In his company, she felt a sense of acceptance and belonging that had been absent for too long, and his unwavering support provided a sense of solace that she had yearned for. With each passing day, it became increasingly clear to Debbie that Ryan held the key to unlocking a sense of peace and contentment that she had thought was beyond her reach.

One evening, as they were engrossed in a heartfelt and lively video chat, Ryan broached the topic of transcending their digital connection and taking the momentous step of meeting in person. The mere suggestion sparked a flurry of emotions within Debbie, as she grappled with a mixture of excitement and nervous anticipation. The prospect of meeting face-to-face with the person who had brought so much joy and companionship into her life was both exhilarating and daunting. As they discussed the logistics and possibilities of an in-person meeting, a whirlwind of thoughts and emotions swirled within Debbie. The idea of bridging the gap between their virtual and physical worlds held the promise of deepening their bond and uncovering new dimensions to their relationship. It was a pivotal moment that filled her with a sense of exhilaration, as she contemplated the potential for their connection to evolve beyond the confines of screens and pixels.

"I know we've only been talking for a few weeks," he said nervously. "But I feel like I already know you so well. I want to see if our connection is just as strong in person."

Debbie's heart skipped a beat at the thought of meeting Ryan face-to-face. She had been hesitant to take their relationship offline at first, but now she couldn't deny her own desire to finally meet him.

"I'd love that," she replied with a smile.

They eagerly made plans to rendezvous at a charming and cozy coffee shop nestled in the heart of their city the following weekend. As the days leading up to their long-awaited meeting passed, Debbie found herself swept up in a whirlwind of emotions, her nerves tingling with a potent blend of excitement and trepidation. The anticipation of their impending date infused each moment with a palpable electricity, as she meticulously prepared for the occasion with meticulous attention to detail, yearning for everything to be perfect. From selecting the ideal outfit that exuded both confidence and comfort to rehearsing casual conversation in front of the mirror, she poured her heart and soul into ensuring that their first face-to-face encounter would be an unforgettable and seamless experience. The prospect of finally meeting Ryan in person ignited a symphony of emotions within Debbie, and she couldn't help but feel a mix of nervousness and exhilaration as she eagerly counted down the days until their much-anticipated rendezvous at the coffee shop.

***

Debbie arrived at the coffee shop early and waited anxiously for Ryan to arrive. When he walked in, her heart fluttered at the sight of him – he was even more handsome in person than he was in his profile pictures.

As they sat across from each other, sipping lattes and talking effortlessly, Debbie thought that this just migh be the start of something special. She felt comfortable and happy with Ryan, something she hadn't felt since before Michael's passing.

After hours of talking and laughing together, Ryan walked Debbie back to her car with a gentle hug goodbye.

"Thank you for tonight," he said softly. "I hope we can do this again."

"I'd like that," Debbie replied, smiling up at him.

*****

The weeks flew by as Debbie and Ryan's relationship continued to grow. They went on more dates, exploring new hiking trails together and attending jazz concerts. Their connection only deepened with each passing day, and it seemed that they were becoming inseparable.

But as much as Debbie wanted to fully embrace her new relationship, she couldn't shake off the lingering guilt she felt towards Michael. She often found herself apologizing to him in her mind for moving on so quickly.

One evening, as they were cuddling on the couch watching a movie, Ryan noticed that something was bothering Debbie.

"Is everything okay?" he asked, stroking her hair gently.

Debbie sighed and looked down at her hands. "I'm just feeling guilty," she admitted. "About us...about moving on."

Ryan's expression softened with understanding. "Debbie, you have nothing to feel guilty about," he reassured her. "Michael will always hold a special place in your heart, but that doesn't mean you can't find happiness again."

"I know," Debbie replied with a sniffle. "I just wish I didn't feel this way."

Ryan leaned in closer and kissed her forehead. "I'll be here for you, no matter what you're feeling. And I promise to help you work through any guilt or doubts that may come up."

Hearing Ryan's heartfelt words of unwavering support and encouragement stirred a mix of emotions within Debbie, causing tears to well up in her eyes as a surge of gratitude and relief washed over her. She found herself enveloped in a warm embrace, her arms wrapping around him tightly as she sought solace in the comfort of his presence. The embrace felt like it served as a testament to the depth of their connection, as their intertwined spirits sought refuge in the shared embrace, transcending the need for words. Her heart was overflowing with a mix of emotions, from the vulnerability of having her feelings laid bare to the overwhelming sense of gratitude for having someone like Ryan by her side. In that embrace, she found reassurance and a renewed sense of strength, knowing that she wasn't alone in facing life's challenges. The tender exchange underscored the profound impact that Ryan's presence had on her, serving as a poignant reminder of the unyielding support and understanding that he unfailingly offered.

"Thank you," she whispered.

***

The following afternoon, Debbie met up with her friends at their favorite café. As they sipped their lattes, she excitedly recounted her conversations with Ryan, her eyes lighting up as she spoke about their shared passions and his seemingly genuine concern for cancer charities.

"Debbie, it sounds like you two have a lot in common, but please be careful," cautioned her friend, Karen. "You know there are people out there who prey on vulnerable individuals like you, especially on these online dating websites."

"Karen's right," chimed in her other friend, Lisa. "We just don't want you to get hurt again. It's important to be cautious and not to invest too much of yourself in someone you've never met."

Debbie nodded, considering their words. She appreciated their concern but couldn't shake the feeling that Ryan was different.

"I understand what you're saying, but I can't help but feel a connection with him. He seems genuine, and I think it's worth taking a chance."

"Alright, Debbie," Karen said gently. "Just remember that we're here for you no matter what. And if anything feels off, please tell us."

"Thank you, both of you," Debbie replied, her heart warmed by their support. As she left the café, the seed of doubt planted by her friends took root, casting a shadow over the hope blossoming within her.

Despite the uncertainty, she knew she needed to pursue this connection with Ryan – not only for the possibility of happiness but also for the chance to honor Michael's memory by making a difference in the fight against cancer.

***

The sun dipped below the horizon, casting an orange glow across Debbie's living room as she sat down at her computer. She hesitated for a moment before opening her email, her heart pounding with a mix of excitement and anxiety. There it was – another message from Ryan.

"Hey Debbie! I hope you're doing well," his email began. "I've been researching some cancer charities lately, but it's hard to know which ones are truly making a difference. I had this crazy idea about starting our own charity to make sure the funds go where they're needed most. What do you think?"

Debbie's eyes widened with surprise and intrigue. The thought of creating a lasting impact in memory of Michael filled her with a renewed sense of purpose. She replied eagerly, expressing her interest and asking for more details about his plan.

Over the course of several emails, Ryan expertly wove his web – sharing stories of cancer survivors who'd been failed by existing charities and lamenting the lack of resources for young people fighting the disease. He painted a vivid picture of the change they could make together, subtly emphasizing the urgency of the situation.

"Debbie, I have to be honest with you. Starting a charity like this requires a fairly substantial initial investment. Not just in time, it needs financing too. I've been saving up for years, but I've ran the numbers and I'm still about 50k short of what we need to really make a difference. I hate to ask, but would you consider contributing some funds to help get this off the ground? I promise every dollar will be put to good use, and you'll be part of something truly meaningful."

Debbie stared at the screen, her fingers hovering over the keyboard. Her heart swelled with the desire to help, but the warning her friends had given her echoed in her mind. Could she trust Ryan? Was this just another online scam?

She took a deep breath and let her thoughts drift back to Michael – the love they'd shared and the hope he'd held onto even in his darkest moments. If there was a chance to make a difference for others like him, wasn't it worth the risk?

"Ryan, I believe in what we're trying to do," she typed hesitantly. "My late husband's life insurance policy left me with some money, and I can't think of a better way to honor his memory than by making a difference in the lives of others fighting cancer."

A wave of emotion washed over Debbie as she hit send. She couldn't shake the feeling that she was teetering on the edge of something monumental.

As she waited for Ryan's response, doubts and fears crept in. What if this was all a scam? What if she was just throwing her hard-earned money away? But then, her thoughts would drift back to Michael and his unwavering determination to make a difference. She knew in her heart that he would want her to take this chance.

Finally, a reply from Ryan appeared in her inbox. He thanked her profusely for her generosity and promised to keep her updated on their progress. He also shared that he had a meeting with potential investors lined up for next week and asked if she would be interested in joining him via video chat.

Debbie's heart raced with excitement at the thought of being a part of this journey from the very beginning. She replied eagerly, agreeing to join the video call.

***

The day of the call arrived and Debbie nervously logged onto the video platform. As soon as Ryan's face appeared on the screen, all her fears melted away. He had a warm smile and an infectious energy that immediately put her at ease.

The other investors joined the call shortly after and Debbie was struck by how passionate they all were about creating a charity that truly made an impact. They discussed their vision, goals, and plans for raising funds. Each person brought unique skills and resources to the table, making Debbie feel like she was part of a powerful team.

At the end of the call, they asked Debbie if she would be willing to contribute not just financially, but also with her time and expertise as a cancer survivor herself. Without hesitation, she agreed.

Debbie's hand trembled as she hovered the cursor above the 'Confirm Transfer' button. The $50,000 she was about to send to Ryan's account seemed like a tangible connection to her late husband, Michael – a part of him that she was entrusting to someone she had never met in person. Her heart raced with a mix of hope and fear, knowing that this could either be her chance at love and a fresh start or a devastating mistake.

"Here goes nothing," she whispered to herself, clicking the button with a mixture of determination and trepidation.

"Transfer Complete" flashed across the screen, and Debbie felt a knot form in her stomach. She immediately sent Ryan a message, letting him know that the funds were on their way.

"Ryan, I've just transferred the money. It's done," she typed hesitantly, her fingers still shaking.

"Debbie, you're amazing! Thank you so much for believing in me and our cause," Ryan replied almost instantly, his words acting as a soothing balm to her anxiety. "I promise you won't regret this. Together, we'll make a real difference in the lives of those battling cancer."

For a brief moment, Debbie allowed herself to revel in the possibility that everything would work out – that they would build something beautiful together in honor of Michael's memory.

However, as the days turned into weeks, Ryan's messages became less frequent and more evasive. He assured her that he was working tirelessly to establish the charity, but something felt off. Gone was the man who shared laughter and heartfelt conversations with her late into the night. In his place was a virtual stranger, distant and cold.

"Hey Ryan, I tried calling you earlier. Can we catch up soon? I miss talking to you," Debbie messaged him one evening after another missed call, her concern growing by the day.

"Sorry, Deb. I've been swamped with work for the charity. You know how it is. I'll call you as soon as I can," came his curt reply.

Debbie couldn't shake the feeling that she was being used and betrayed. The seed of doubt her friends had planted had morphed into a gnawing suspicion that she'd made a terrible mistake – one that could cost her more than just money.

As Ryan's silence stretched on, Debbie's heartache turned to anger, fueled by the realization that she might never see the $50,000 again. She refused to be a victim of deceit any longer. If Ryan thought he could take advantage of her vulnerability and slip away without consequence, he was sorely mistaken.

"Enough is enough," she murmured through gritted teeth, vowing to take action and reclaim what was stolen from her – and perhaps, in the process, heal the wounds left by betrayal and loss.

***

Debbie sat in her living room, the harsh light of her laptop screen casting eerie shadows on her face as she scoured the internet for answers. Her eyes widened as she stumbled upon a webpage filled with stories strikingly similar to her own – tales of heartbreak and deceit at the hands of online scammers.

"Romance fraud," she whispered, her voice cracking under the weight of her newfound knowledge. A mixture of anger and determination surged through her veins, propelling her towards action. If there was one thing she knew, it was that she couldn't let Ryan get away with what he had done. She owed it to herself, and to others who might fall prey to his charm in the future.

"Enough is enough," she murmured, fingers flying across the keyboard as she searched for help. One name kept popping up in her search results: Nathaniel "Nate" Everhart and Amelia "Amy" Everhart, a husband and wife team with a reputation for helping people track down and confront scammers. With nothing left to lose, Debbie typed out an email to them, pouring out her story and begging for their assistance.

You are Debbie. Your husband died from cancer and you recieved $50,000 from his life insurance. You met a man online somewhat recently called Ryan. You and Ryan got on well. Ryan told you he was starting a cancer charity and asked you for an investment of $50,000 towards the startup costs. You sent him the $50,000. He ghosted you after that. Romance fraud. You have been the victim of romance fraud. You find a couple, Nathaniel and Amelia who are like a modern day A-Team that might be able to help you. Write an email to Nathaniel and Amelia seeking their assistance.

Subject: Seeking Your Help Against Romance Fraud

Dear Nathaniel and Amelia,

I hope this message finds you well. My name is Debbie, and I recently found myself in a distressing situation that I believe requires the expertise of individuals like yourselves. I was the victim of a romance fraud, and I am reaching out to you in the hope that you might be able to help me.

After losing my husband to cancer, I received a life insurance payout of $50,000. In the midst of coping with this loss, I met a man named Ryan online, and we formed a connection. Ryan shared with me his ambitious plan to start a cancer charity and asked for an investment of $50,000 to cover the startup costs. Believing in his cause and feeling a connection with him, I entrusted him with the entire sum.

However, after I sent him the money, Ryan vanished without a trace. It became clear to me that I had fallen victim to romance fraud, and I have been left in a state of emotional and financial turmoil.

In my search for assistance, I came across your reputation as a modern-day A-Team, and I am hopeful that you might be able to help me navigate this distressing situation. I am in need of guidance, support, and potentially even intervention to seek justice and recover from this devastating experience.

I would be deeply grateful for the chance to discuss my situation with you further and explore any potential avenues for recourse.

Thank you for taking the time to read my message, and I hope to hear from you soon.

Best regards, Debbie

Debbie's hands trembled as she clicked the send button on her email to Nate and Amy Everhart. She had laid out all the details of her relationship with Ryan, from their initial meeting online to his sudden disappearance and her suspicions of his fraudulent intentions.

She hoped they would be able to help her track him down and get her money back, but more than that, she wanted closure. She couldn't let this go without a fight.

Days went by with no response from neither Nate nor Amy. Debbie was starting to lose hope when finally, an email from them arrived in her inbox.

Dear Debbie,

Thank you for reaching out to us. We have read your story and we understand how difficult this must be for you. We would like to help you in any way we can.

Firstly, please know that you are not alone in this.

Unfortunately, there are many people who have fallen victim to romance scams like the one you experienced. Many of them have come to us for assistance and we have been able to track down the scammers and bring them to justice.

We will need some additional information from you in order to start our investigation. Please provide us with any emails or messages you have exchanged with Ryan, as well as any photos or documents he may have sent you. Also, if possible, the name or contact information of the charity he claimed to be creating would be helpful.

Sincerely,

Nate and Amy.

Tears streamed down Debbie's face as she read their words. It was a glimmer of hope in what had seemed like an endless pit of despair.

She quickly gathered all the evidence she had and sent it off to Nate and Amy. They responded promptly, acknowledging receipt of the materials and assuring her that they would begin their investigation immediately.

The next day, she received a FaceTime call. After a moment's hesitation, she answered with audio only.

"Hello?" she said nervously.

"Hi, Debbie? This is Nate Everhart." His voice was warm, inviting trust. "We're sorry to hear about what you've been through, and we want to help you."

Debbie's shaking fingertip slid across the screen as she enabled video for the call. She held her phone tightly, feeling the smooth metal casing against her sweaty palm.

"Thank you," Debbie choked out, tears welling up in her eyes. "I just... I don't know where else to turn. I can't believe I fell for it."

"Hey, don't blame yourself," Nate reassured her. "These scammers are professionals at what they do. It's not your fault."

"Exactly," Amy chimed in, her voice equally reassuring. "And we're going to do everything we can to help you get your money back and bring this guy to justice."

"Thank you both so much," Debbie whispered, the sound of hope returning to her voice.

Nate and Amy exchanged a glance, their eyes meeting briefly before they turned their attention back to Debbie's tearful face on the screen. The weight of her story hung in the air, pulling at the corners of their smiles, as they sat in their shared home office.

"Look," Nate began cautiously, rubbing the back of his neck, "I'll be honest with you, Debbie. Romance scams are tricky, and trying to track down someone like Ryan isn't going to be easy. There are risks involved that we need to consider."

Debbie's heart constricted as she sensed their hesitation, but she refused to let her hope dissipate. "I understand if you don't want to take my case," she said, her voice barely above a whisper, "but I can't just sit here and do nothing. I need closure, and I do need your help."

Amy's gaze softened as she recognized the desperation in Debbie's eyes – a mirror image of her own when she fought to clear her father's name. "Debbie," she said gently, "we know how important this is to you, so we'll do everything we can to help. But you need to understand that there are no guarantees. Are you willing to accept that?"

Debbie nodded, biting her lip. "Yes," she murmured, feeling both grateful and terrified.

"Alright then," Nate said, his tone shifting from skeptical to resolute. "Let's get to work."

"Remember, Debbie," Nate said, his fingers dancing over the keyboard as he prepared to dive into the digital world, "our goal is to outsmart Ryan at his own game. We're not just going to beat him; we're going to make him wish he'd never crossed your path."

Debbie's pulse quickened as she heard the determination in Nate's voice, the unwavering strength and resolve that seemed to radiate from him, filling the room with an almost palpable energy. She found herself caught between admiration for their expertise and fear of what lay ahead, her mind racing with a whirlwind of emotions. The realization of just how deeply she had become entangled in this web of deceit sent shivers down her spine, and yet, in the presence of Nate and Amy, she felt a glimmer of hope beginning to bloom within her. Their confidence was infectious, their unwavering commitment to helping her reclaim what had been taken from her was nothing short of awe-inspiring. As she gazed at them, she couldn't help but marvel at the sheer strength and resilience they exuded, like a beacon of light cutting through the darkness that had clouded her world.

"Thank you," she said, her voice trembling with emotion, her eyes glistening with unshed tears. "I don't know what I would do without you two. You've given me hope in the darkest of times, and I will be forever grateful for your support."

Amy smiled at Debbie through the screen, her eyes filled with empathy and conviction. "We'll get through this together," she assured her. "And when we're done, you'll be the one smiling."

Debbie gazed at the screen, her eyes fixed on the digital images that held the promise of reclaiming what had been taken from her. Her heart raced in her chest, a mix of fear and hope coursing through her veins, like conflicting currents pulling her in different directions. The anxiety of the unknown future clashed against the glimmer of optimism that Nate and Amy's intervention offered. She clutched a frayed tissue in one hand, the delicate fabric a tangible anchor in the storm of emotions swirling within her. The other hand instinctively found solace in gripping her late husband's gold ring that hung from a delicate chain around her neck, the weight of the metal a comforting reminder of the love and strength she carried with her. In that quiet moment, sitting alone in her dimly lit living room, the presence of the ring served as a bittersweet connection to the past and a source of resilience as she ventured into an uncertain future.

"Okay, Debbie," Nate began, his voice steady and reassuring. "I think we have a semblance of a plan a strategy to track down Ryan and recover your money. It won't be easy, and we will need to call in someone else to assist, but we're going to do everything in our power to make this right."

Amy chimed in, her red hair shimmering like fire as she nodded in agreement. "And we won't rest until justice is served, and you can finally put this nightmare behind you."

Debbie swallowed hard, the lump in her throat making it difficult to speak. She could feel the weight of her late husband's gold ring hanging from the chain around her neck, a tangible reminder of the love and loss she had experienced. Her fingers tightened around the ring, seeking comfort in its familiar presence as she struggled to contain the whirlwind of emotions swirling within her. "Tell me what I need to do," she said, her voice wavering with determination, a glimmer of resilience shining through the cracks of her vulnerability. The sense of urgency and desperation in her tone was unmistakable, a reflection of the tumultuous journey she had endured, and the unwavering resolve to seek justice and reclaim what had been taken from her.

Nate leaned forward, his dark eyes locked on the camera. "First, we'll need you to gather any information or evidence you have about your interactions with Ryan. Emails, text messages, anything that could help us identify patterns or specific details he might've overlooked."

Amy continued, outlining other aspects of the plan: coordinating with law enforcement, tracing financial transactions, and even employing some of Nate's hacking skills if necessary. With each new revelation, Debbie felt a renewed sense of hope, her trust in Nate and Amy's abilities growing stronger.

"Lastly," Amy said, her tone taking on a more solemn note, "we need to be prepared for the possibility that Ryan will retaliate once he realizes we're onto him. We'll do everything we can to protect you, Debbie, but it's important that you understand the risks involved."

Debbie's hands trembled as she considered the potential danger she was putting herself in. The weight of her decision settled heavily on her shoulders, causing her to take a deep breath to steady herself. She glanced at the framed photo of her late husband, a pang of sadness and longing washing over her. But then she thought of the $50,000 she'd lost, the hard-earned money that had been cruelly snatched away from her through deceit and manipulation. The memory of Ryan's smooth-talking charm and false promises ignited a fire within her, fueling her determination to seek justice and ensure that he would not get away with his crimes. No, she couldn't let Ryan go unpunished. The thought of others falling victim to his schemes, losing their savings and experiencing the same heartache she had endured, propelled her forward. It wasn't just about recovering her own funds; it was about putting an end to his reign of deception and protecting others from falling into the same trap. With every fiber of her being, she resolved to stand up, fight back, and reclaim not only her money but her dignity as well.

"I understand," she whispered, her voice firm with resolve. "I want to do this. For my husband, for myself... and for anyone else he might prey on in the future."

"Debbie, we'll be with you every step of the way," Nate assured her, his words carrying the weight of a solemn promise. "We've faced people like Ryan before, and we won't let him get away with what he's done."

"Thank you," Debbie murmured, her eyes filling with tears of gratitude. "I don't know how I can ever repay you both."

"Seeing you regain your life and find closure is all the repayment we need," Amy replied gently, her own eyes shining with empathy.

As the conversation drew to a close, Debbie felt a newfound determination surge within her. The road ahead would be difficult, filled with challenges and uncertainty. But with Nate and Amy by her side, she was ready to face whatever lay ahead – and reclaim what had been taken from her.

Chapter 1

Chapter 2

The steady hum of computer fans filled the dimly lit home office as Nate and Amy hunched over their respective screens. Papers littered the desk, a chaotic mosaic of schematics, research, and notes scribbled with determination. The glow of the monitors cast eerie shadows on their faces as they exchanged glances, both knowing they were at a critical point in their mission.

"Alright," Nate said, rubbing his tired eyes. "We need someone to play a part. We've got you as the customer service rep, I'll take the FCA role, but who as the CIA? Finding people, accessing computer or CCTV systems, I can do that but I'm not good at switching voices. We need help."

Amy sighed, her fingers gripping the edge of the table as she contemplated their dilemma. "I know, but who can we trust with something like this? It's risky, and we can't afford any mistakes."

Nate leaned back in his chair, drumming his fingers on the armrests. His mind raced through names and faces, each one falling short of the skills and connections they needed. Then, a spark of inspiration hit him. "Logan," he blurted out, the name echoing around the room.

"Logan?" Amy repeated, her eyebrows knitting together in concern. "You mean that street hustler you met while working undercover years ago?"

"Exactly," Nate replied, leaning forward with excitement. "He's smart, cunning, and has pulled off some pretty elaborate schemes in his time. Plus, he'll love doing this. I think he could be invaluable in helping us get to Ryan and recovering Debbie's money."

Amy's lips were pressed together in a thin line as she nibbled on her bottom lip, her eyes scanning Nate's face for any sign of hesitation or doubt. Her green eyes were furrowed in concentration, studying the lines and creases on his face for any hint of uncertainty. Her fingers fidgeted with the fabric of her shirt, a nervous habit that betrayed her anxiety.

She knew her husband was skilled at reading people, but Logan was an unknown variable. She couldn't shake the nagging worry in the pit of her stomach.

"Are you sure about this?" Amy asked, her voice wavering slightly. "Can we really trust him?"

"Look, I know Logan's been on the wrong side of the law more times than we can count," Nate admitted. "But when it comes down to it, he's loyal to his friends and has a code of ethics. He won't screw us over, I promise."

Amy hesitated for a moment longer before finally nodding in agreement. "Alright, if you think he's our best shot, let's reach out to him. But be careful, Nate. We're putting a lot on the line here, and I don't want anything to go wrong."

"Don't worry," Nate reassured her, a determined glint in his eye. "With Logan on our side, there's no way Ryan stands a chance. We'll recover Debbie's money and make sure he pays for what he's done."

As they returned their focus to the computer screens, the gravity of their mission weighed heavily on their shoulders. They knew the risks, but they were driven by the desire to bring justice to those who preyed on the vulnerable. With Logan's help, they hoped to tip the odds in their favor and finally take down the charming predator known as Ryan Anderson.

Amy's fingers were tapping rapidly on the edge of the desk, her nails digging into the wood with each nervous movement. Her eyes darted back and forth between Nate and the computer screens, her brows furrowed in deep concentration. The worry lines on her forehead were visible as she bit her bottom lip, her gaze flickering with uncertainty. Her stomach twisted in knots, causing her to shift uncomfortably in her seat. The tension in the room was palpable as they considered reaching out to Logan for help.

"Are you sure about this?" she asked, her voice wavering slightly. "Can we really trust him?"

Nate leaned back in his chair, his gaze steady as he met Amy's concerned eyes. "Look, I know Logan's been on the wrong side of the law more times than we can count," he admitted. "But when it comes down to it, he's loyal to his friends and has a code of ethics. He won't screw us over, I promise. With Logan on our side, there's no way Ryan stands a chance, assuming we play our parts well enough. We'll recover Debbie's money and make sure he pays for what he's done."

As Amy watched Nate pull out his phone and dial Logan's number, she couldn't help but feel a mix of excitement and fear. This was it. They were all in now, and there was no turning back.

Amy held her breath as she watched Nate wait for Logan to answer the call. The suspense was almost too much to bear, and she couldn't help but fidget in her seat. After what felt like an eternity, Nate's face broke into a relieved smile as he heard Logan's voice on the other end.

"Hey, Logan, it's Nate," Nate began, his voice cool and casual. "Listen, I've got a proposition for you. Something that might interest you."

"Everhart, huh?" Logan replied, his voice laced with suspicion. "You two are playing with fire these days, aren't you? What's in it for me?"

"Well, there's a pretty big payday involved," Nate explained, trying to appeal to Logan's love of money. "But more importantly, we're taking down a real scumbag. You know, the kind that preys on vulnerable people? We could use your skills and connections."

"Look, Nate," Logan said hesitantly, "I'm not gonna lie. This sounds risky, and I've been trying to keep my head down lately. What you're proposing... It ain't exactly legal, is it?"

"Legal?" Nate chuckled. "Well, let's just say our target isn't exactly playing by the rules either. We're just leveling the playing field, and ensuring justice is served. He's not going to grass because it's money he stole. We're stealing it back and giving it back to the person he stole it from. It's good karma, Logan."

Amy's eyes were wide as she stared at the phone in Nate's hand. She nervously bit her lip, her fingers tapping anxiously on her thigh. Her body was tense, and she seemed to be physically holding her breath, waiting for Logan's response. A look of determination and hope mixed on her face as she watched Nate speak, desperately wishing for Logan to agree.

"Alright," Logan sighed after a pause. "I'll hear you out. But if I don't like what I hear, I'm out. Got it?"

"Fair enough," Nate replied, relief evident in his voice. "We'll discuss the details when we meet up. You won't regret this."

The sun cast long shadows across the room as Nate and Amy sat huddled together, their faces illuminated by the glow of the computer screen. They knew that time was running out to recover Debbie's money, and that they needed Logan's expertise if they were going to bring Ryan down. With a deep breath, Nate dialed Logan's number and waited for him to pick up.

"Hey, Logan," Nate began, his voice calm and collected. "We want to make sure you understand that we're only going after scammers and fraudsters who prey on vulnerable people like Debbie. We're not looking to cause trouble for anyone who doesn't deserve it."

"Those people deserve to be taken down a peg or two," Amy chimed in, her determination shining through. "And we need someone with your skills to make it happen."

Logan hesitated, clearly weighing his options. "This whole thing is risky, and I don't want to get myself in too deep."

Nate leaned back in his chair, rubbing his temple as he considered his next words. "Logan, think about it. You've got the chance to help right a wrong here. Not many people get that opportunity, especially in our line of work. And besides," he added with a grin, "you know you love a good challenge."

Amy could sense Logan wavering on the other end of the line. She decided to play the empathy card. "Imagine if it was someone you cared about who lost everything because of a scammer like Ryan," she said softly. "Wouldn't you want justice for them?"

There was a moment of silence before Logan let out a resigned sigh. "Alright, fine. But if things start to go south, I'm out."

"Deal," Nate agreed. "We'll meet you at that coffee shop on the corner of Main and Elm in an hour."

"See you there," Logan replied, hanging up.

As Nate hung up the phone, he exchanged a determined look with Amy. They had secured their wildcard, and now it was time to put their plan into action. Together, they would bring Ryan Anderson's criminal empire crashing down around him, and secure Debbie's future once and for all. The stakes were high, but so were the potential rewards, and they wouldn't back down until justice was served.

***

As Nate and Amy entered the bustling café, they spotted Logan sitting near the back, nursing a cup of black coffee. They slid into the booth across from him and exchanged tense greetings.

"Alright," Logan said, folding his arms across his chest. "What's this big plan of yours?"

Nate took a deep breath, ready to lay out every detail of their scheme. He knew that this was their one shot to convince Logan to join them, and he couldn't afford to let it slip through their fingers.

"First, we need to gather a bit of intel on Ryan" Nate began. "That shouldn't be too hard. I have a photo of him in his living room with a window behind him. From that, we can figure out exactly where he is, even easier if the image has meta data actually telling us the coordinates of where the shot was taken."

"Then, we just call him and ask for the money," Amy added with a smile. "We won't immediately ask for it. We'll social engineer him to hand us the money."

Logan listened closely, his eyes narrowing as he processed the information. "Where do I come in?" he asked.

"You Sir, are the icing on the cake. Amy lures him in, I soften him up," Nate explained. "Then you take the call and he should be just about ready to go to the bank and pick up the money for us."

A tense silence hung in the air as Logan mulled over the proposal. Finally, he nodded slowly. "Alright, I'm in. But remember, if anything goes wrong, I'm holding you two responsible."

"Understood," Nate replied, extending his hand for a firm shake. "Now let's get to work."

The clinking sound of coffee cups and the faint aroma of freshly ground beans filled the air as Logan leaned back in his chair, evaluating Nate and Amy with a cautious eye. "Before we go any further, I need to make one thing clear," he said, his voice firm yet quiet enough not to draw attention from nearby patrons. "I have my own code of ethics. I don't target innocent people, and I have no intention of getting involved in anything that crosses that line."

Nate nodded, understanding the gravity of Logan's statement. "We're on the same page, Logan. Our plan is only aimed at Ryan and his dirty money. Debbie's just an innocent victim caught in his web, and we want to make sure she gets her money back."

"Exactly," Amy chimed in. "This really is more the A-Team than Robin Hood. Our goal is to protect vulnerable individuals like Debbie while ensuring justice is served to people like Ryan who prey on them."

Logan's gaze flicked between the two, searching for any hint of deception. After a moment, he seemed satisfied and relaxed slightly. "Alright then, let's hear the details."

Nate took a sip of his coffee, gathering his thoughts before laying out their plan. "Debbie gave us a photo of him in his living room with a window in the background. From that, we should be able to figure out where he lives. If we run into any problems, we'll call Jose Monkey, that's his thing and he's the best in world at finding locations from very little information. We have his cell phone number, but we need his address. I'll do a physical recce of the location and confirm it's him living there."

"Once we have those details," Amy chimed, "then it's game on. I'll call him pretending to be from Amazon support and tell him we need to confirm some unusual transactions. Some big ticket items."

"He'll say he didn't purchase them," Nate said.

"Of course he'll say that, because he didn't order the items," Amy continued. "I'll tell him it was from his business account. An account that he also doesn't have. Then we convince him that he's been the victim of identity theft, that we've seen a spate of them recently and I will forward him to the FTC who are looking into these cases for us. That's where Nate comes in."

"Yup," Nate said, taking over. "We respond the number of the FTC and I claim there is quite a case built around him: several million dollars, some sort of drug deal etc. and he's in deep shit."

Logan leaned back in his chair, taking another sip of the strong coffee provided by Nate and Amy. His mind was racing with the intricacies of their plan to take down Ryan and get Debbie's money back.

"So, what do you need from me?" he finally asked, breaking the silence.

Nate and Amy exchanged glances before turning back to Logan. "He's in deep shit and the CIA are looking into it," Nate continued. "That's where you come in. I can't do voices, so we need another person in on the scam."

"Let me guess," Logan said, twirling a tea spoon in his fingers. "I'm the CIA."

"One of them, yes," Amy said.

"One of them? You have more people roped in on this?" Logan asked, surprised.

"No, no," Amy laughed.

"I'll play the other CIA agent," Nate declared.

"But I thought you said you were no good with voices."

"It's a non speaking part, and later in the day. We've softened him up and you just come in heavy with Federal crime charges and make him go to the bank. I'm the 'undercover' agent that picks the money up 'for safekeeping and to stop him getting charged."

"Sounds pretty elaborate," Nate replied.

Amy jumped in, "It is. That's why it needs the 3 of us. It's based on a Social Engineering scam that actually happened a while back to someone who thought she was too clever to be scammed in such a way. The situation escalates rapidly by tightening the thumb screws just a bit each time, making the scenario believable based on previous data. Which, of course, wasn't honest data."

"I like it!" Logan exclaimed. "I'm so in"."

"We thought you might be," replied Nate. "We figured you'd be the perfect guy to do this and you'd be great at it. The good karma bit is that we're only taking money that was wrongfully stolen and returning it to the person it was stolen from."

"Like some sort of Robin Hood?" Logan asked.

"Sort of," answered Amy. "Except we wouldn't be stealing from the rich to give to the poor. We'd be stealing from the thief to give back to the thieved. Did you ever see an episode of The A-Team from back in the 80s? I think they made a movie about it at the end of the noughties. More like that really."

"Yeah, I reckon it is," Logan replied, nodding. Logan's eyes shone with excitement at the thought of being involved in such an elaborate and daring scheme.

Nate leaned back in his chair, a solemn expression on his face as he acknowledged Logan's potential concerns. "We understand your hesitation, Logan. But we've meticulously planned every step of this mission." He locked eyes with Logan, exuding an air of confidence that seemed to put the hustler at ease. "Amy and I have worked together on numerous operations like this one. Our combined skills and experience more than qualify us to pull this off."

Logan took a deep breath, his fingers drumming on the table as he mulled over their words. He knew they were skilled, but the stakes were high, and he was worried about the possible fallout from their actions. The thought of prison loomed in his mind, casting a dark shadow over his thoughts.

"Look," Nate continued, sensing Logan's trepidation, "we've got your back, just like you'll have ours. We're in this together, and we won't let anything happen to you. Trust us."

Logan hesitated for a moment longer before finally nodding, his resolve wavering but ultimately strengthened by their assurances. "Alright. I trust you guys," he said, the words carrying the weight of his commitment. "Let's do this."

A collective breath was released, and the trio dove back into their planning, the energy in the room charged with a renewed sense of purpose. They knew they were taking a few risks, but with their combined skills and determination, nothing would stand in their way.

Logan's thoughts raced as they discussed each aspect of the operation, mentally reviewing potential scenarios and contingencies. He knew there was no room for error – not when lives and reputations were on the line.

"Remember, our primary goal is to recover Debbie's money," Nate reminded everyone, his tone firm yet laced with an underlying current of empathy. "We're not doing this for personal gain. We're doing it for justice."

"Agreed," Logan nodded, the conviction in his voice matching Nate's. "It's time for Ryan to pay for the consequences."

"Then it's settled," Amy said, her eyes gleaming with determination. "We'll meet again tomorrow to finalize everything and begin putting our plan into action. Stay sharp and stay focused – we can't afford to slip up now."

As the trio made their way out of the cozy coffee shop, Logan's heart began to beat faster with a surge of anticipation and a hint of nervousness. The bustling city street ahead seemed to pulsate with energy, its neon signs and bright lights casting a colorful glow onto the pavement. Logan felt a mix of excitement and hesitation as they ventured into the unknown, ready for whatever adventure lay ahead.

Chapter 3

The dimly lit room was alive with the hum of computer monitors, a soft glow casting eerie shadows on Amy's face as she prepared for the call. Her workspace, cluttered with scraps of paper covered in hastily scribbled notes, was testament to her relentless dedication. With her striking red hair tied back in a tight bun, she leaned in toward the mirror and rehearsed her lines one more time, her lips moving silently.

"Amazon customer service... unusual activity... here to help," she muttered to herself, adjusting the headset that hugged her ears. Her attention to detail had always been an indispensable part of the team, and this call was no exception. She straightened her spine, rolled her shoulders back, and took a deep breath, drawing upon the calm demeanor that had served her well in the past. Her investigative journalism background held her in good stead; it had taught her how to adapt quickly to changing circumstances and think on her feet when needed.

With a couple of taps, Nate spoofed the caller-id for outgoing calls. A sly grin spread across his face. Now, whenever he made a call, the number would appear to come from Amazon.

"Showtime," Amy whispered under her breath, her heart pounding with anticipation as she dialed Ryan's number. The sound of the ringing phone echoed through the room, each tone heightening the tension that crackled like electricity in the air. She could feel her pulse quicken, but she remained focused, her mind razor-sharp.

"Please pick up," she thought, her fingers tapping a nervous rhythm on the desk. Each ring was a countdown, a reminder that there was no turning back now. This was the moment they had been working towards, the crucial first step in their elaborate scam plan. And she was ready.

"Hello?" came the voice on the other end, smooth and unsuspecting. Ryan Anderson had answered, and it was showtime indeed.

"Hello, Mr Anderson? This is Amy from Amazon Customer Service," she began, her voice calm and professional. "I'm calling you today because we've noticed some unusual activity on your account that has raised a few red flags for us. The system flags these as potential security issues, requiring us to call and confirm the transactions."

Ryan's smooth voice tried to hide the hint of concern that crept in as he responded. "Oh, really? What kind of unusual activity?"

Amy continued, her tone steady and reassuring. "Well, first I must assure you that this call is being recorded for training purposes but there have been multiple high-value purchases in fairly rapid succession. It's not typical behavior for your account, so we need to just confirm the transactions."

"Uh, okay... Thanks for letting me know," Ryan said, his curiosity piqued. "What do we need to do to fix this?"

"First, I will need to verify some information with you," Amy replied, sticking to the script they had rehearsed.

"Can you confirm that your last name is Anderson?" Amy asked.

"Anderson, yes," Ryan confirmed. "What sort of transactions?"

"Sorry Mr. Anderson, I just need to confirm that I am speaking with the correct person, some of the details may be personal or sensitive and we wouldn't want the information in the wrong hands. You are Ryan Anderson, is that correct?"

"Yes, that's correct."

"Could you please, just this last question, confirm your Amazon ID email address?"

Ryan told Amy his email address which, of course, Amy already knew.

Amy felt a sense of satisfaction at how easily Ryan seemed to be buying into their ruse.

Once they had finished verifying Ryan's information, Amy smoothly transitioned to the next step.

"Thank you, Ryan. I appreciate your cooperation. The transactions in question relate to several purchases made yesterday amounting to $8,426.32, some MacBooks and ancillary computer equipment."

Ryan quickly logged into his Amazon account and looked at his order history. Nothing was out of the ordinary, certainly no new MacBooks purchased yesterday.

"No, I didn't order them and they're not in my order history," he replied.

"We put a hold on the transactions until we could verify them, Mr. Anderson, they wouldn't show in your order history. They were on your business account."

"Yeah, I don't have a business account at Amazon," Ryan said, clearly there was an error somewhere.

"Our system says that you actually have 2 business accounts," Amy said, sticking loosely to the script. She paused before continuing, as if she was weighing up what should be done. "I'll be honest with you Mr. Anderson, we've seen a spate of similar transactions across the business recently and, because of the high rate of identity theft, the FTC have been involved."

Ryan's words were laced with uncertainty as he questioned, "The FTC? Is this serious?" His voice wavered, betraying his growing concern.

"Yes, I'm afraid it is," Amy replied solemnly. "But don't worry, we're here to help you through this. My team has been working closely with the Federal Trade Commission and have a direct connection to them. The reference number for this case is 5234572, feel free to write it down, but it will be emailed to you in due course. I'll transfer the call to the FTC who can provide you with more information about the situation, provide assistance and explain what steps you need to take. Please stay on the line while I transfer you."

Ryan's mind was swirling with confusion. He had always been meticulous about his Amazon orders, yet now there were accusations of something wrong with his account. The mention of a business account only added to his bewilderment. He couldn't recall ever setting one up and the involvement of the FTC made the situation feel much more serious. Was someone using his name for their own gain? He knew he needed to get to the bottom of this, but his thoughts were in turmoil as he tried to piece together what could have gone wrong.

Nate converted the caller-id to the number of the FTC.

As the call connected to Nate, Amy watched him take a deep breath, his chest expanding as he prepared to speak. He cleared his throat, and when he began talking, his voice was authoritative and commanding, leaving no room for doubt that he was a man of importance.

"Hello, Ryan," Nate said, smoothly taking over the call. "My name is Agent Nathaniel Everhart with the Federal Trade Commission. This call is being recorded. Your call has been transferred to me from Amazon." Nate paused, as if to be reading from a screen. "I'm just cross referencing these transactions and your details with our database. Our data goes a bit deeper, Amazon only has record of the transactions within Amazon. Bear with me one moment."

Nate made some random mouse clicks and noisy keyboard presses for about 20 seconds. "Sorry to alarm you Mr. Anderson, but we have reason to believe your personal information has been compromised and used fraudulently by an organised crime gang creating multiple accounts and linked to both substantial drug dealing and money laundering. Are you familiar with reportfraud.ftc.gov[1]?" Nate didn't wait for an answer. "This is a very serious situation, and I need to emphasize the potential legal consequences you could face if this is not resolved."

Ryan's voice shook as he tried to make sense of the overwhelming situation before him. "This can't be happening... What am I supposed to do now? Is there even a way to fix this mess?" His mind raced with conflicting thoughts and emotions, unsure of what steps to take next.

Nate smiled. Ryan was hooked, thanks in large part to Amy and her wonderful portrayal of a concerned Amazon customer service agent.

---

1.   http://reportfraud.ftc.gov/

Nate reassured Ryan, his tone firm yet empathetic. "We're working on it, Ryan. Our main priority is catching the culprits and protecting your identity. But we'll need your full cooperation to ensure this matter is resolved quickly and effectively."

"We've tracked this criminal activity to a gang known as the Black Vipers. They're notorious for identity theft and using stolen information to help fund their extensive drug operations," Nate explained, his voice steady and convincing. "We recently intercepted messages between members of this gang discussing a 'new gold mine,' which we believe is referring to your personal information. There are a number of accounts in your name, funds sent abroad and ... oh," Nate paused for effect.

"What is it?" Ryan asked apprehensively.

Nate paused for a moment, allowing the weight of his words to sink in before ignoring Ryan's question. He lowered the pitch of his voice and spoke a little slower, adding gravitas to what he was about to say. "Now, I need you to think carefully, Ryan. Have you noticed any unusual activity lately? Any strange emails, phone calls, or people following you?"

Ryan hesitated, his mind racing. "I...I did get some odd emails last week, but I just thought they were spam. And there was a guy who seemed to be watching me when I left work a few days ago..."

"Alright," Nate said, his tone reassuring. "That could very well be connected. Rest assured, we're doing everything in our power to catch these criminals and protect your identity. But time is of the essence, so we need your full cooperation."

"Of course, anything you need," Ryan replied, his voice wavering slightly.

"Thank you, Ryan. At this point, I'm going to bring in one of my colleagues from the CIA. He's been tracking the Black Vipers for quite some time and will have more information about how to proceed. Please hold on while I transfer the call."

Nate converted the caller ID to the main number of the CIA and passed the call over to Logan.

As Ryan answered the call from Logan, his heart began to race. He could hear the authority and certainty in Logan's voice.

"Good evening, Ryan. My name is Agent Logan Brown with the Central Intelligence Agency, badge number 956. This call is being recorded. I understand you've just been speaking with my colleague at the FTC about your case."

Ryan's mind raced, trying to remember details about the conversation he'd only just had.

"Yes, yes I have," Ryan replied, his anxiety palpable.

"I have the details on the screen in front of me," Logan continued, his tone authoritative yet persuasive. "I've been working on this case for several months now, and I can assure you, we're closing in on the Black Vipers. However, your situation is quite precarious."

Ryan's throat tightened as he fought to swallow back the fear rising in his chest. He could feel his mouth going dry, his tongue sticking to the roof of his mouth. Dread washed over him as he whispered, "What do you mean?"

"Simply put, Ryan, you're in deep trouble," Logan said, using his street smarts to gauge Ryan's reaction. "This gang is relentless, and won't hesitate to eliminate anyone who gets in their way. We need to act fast if we want to keep you safe and bring these criminals to justice."

As the gravity of the situation dawned on Ryan, he realized just how critical it was to trust the people who were trying to help him. With his heart pounding and his mind racing, he knew he had no choice but to follow their lead - no matter where it took him.

"Ryan, listen to me," Logan began, his voice steady but urgent. "They obviously have access your bank accounts and can extract any funds you have in there. We need you to move your money to a secure location until we catch them."

"Move my money? Where?" Ryan asked, his voice wavering with concern.

"Somewhere safe. Don't worry. We have a process for this sort of thing. How much money do you have available? Bear in mind that anything left in your accounts can be seized."

Ryan's heart pounded in his chest as he faced the possibility of losing everything. The weight of his financial decisions bore down on him, threatening to crush him completely. His eyes darted to the account balance, reading the staggering number: $55,246. "Not much over fifty five," he said.

"Fifty five what, Ryan? Fifty five dollars? fifty five hundred dollars? Let's not waste time here, literally every second counts," Logan said rather aggressively.

Nate nodded approvingly, he new Logan was the right man for the job from day one.

"Fifty five thousand. Dollars. Fifty five thousand dollars," Ryan answered, his voice shaking a little.

"Right," Logan said, "I need you to go to the bank and withdraw $50,000 in cash. Don't say anything that might alert the teller in any way. On one of my cases, the teller was the bad guy. Trust no-one Ryan, anyone could be someone sent to watch you."

Ryan's mind raced with doubt and suspicion "I don't know... This all sounds too... strange. How do I know this isn't some sort of scam? That you're not spoofing the phone number"

"I understand your skepticism, Ryan," Logan replied, employing his persuasive skills. "But this is a government number, it can't be spoofed."

Ryan wasn't sure how true that was and started to google it, but Logan immediately continued:

"Right now, time is of the essence. The longer you wait, the greater the risk that these criminals will get their hands on your hard-earned money. You have my word as a CIA agent that we will keep you safe. You have my badge number and this call is being recorded."

As Ryan processed Logan's words, he could feel the desperation closing in on him. His throat constricted, making it difficult to speak. He knew that if he didn't act quickly, he might lose everything. But trusting these strangers over the phone was a leap of faith that left him feeling vulnerable and exposed.

"Can you guarantee my safety?" Ryan finally managed to ask, his voice barely audible.

"Ryan, I promise you that we will do everything in our power to protect you and your assets. We've been tracking the Black Vipers for months, and we're closing in on them. All we need is your cooperation," Logan said, his tone leaving no room for doubt.

With his back against the wall, Ryan felt the weight of the decision pressing down on him. He took a deep breath, his heart pounding in his chest. As much as he wanted to dismiss the situation as a hoax, the genuine concern in Logan's voice was hard to ignore. And so, with his hands trembling and his mind racing, Ryan made a choice that would change the course of his life forever.

"Alright," Ryan said, his voice wavering with relief and gratitude. "Thank you. I appreciate your help. I'll do whatever it takes to protect my money and myself."

"Good," Logan replied, his voice firm and reassuring. "Now listen very carefully." Logan lowered the timbre of his voice a little before continuing. "The safest way for us to keep your money safe is for the CIA to secure your funds as cash in an evidence locker then issue you a Government check so that there is a solid transaction proving that the money was yours when we take these guys to Federal Court. What I need you to do is go to the bank and withdraw the $50,000 in cash. Do not, let me repeat that, do not alert the bank staff in any way. In one case I worked on, one of the bank staff was part of the group and it blew our cover and put the victim in serious danger. We don't want that to happen to you, so remain calm and do not alert the bank staff. It's for your safety as well as the case."

Logan paused. "Do you understand so far?"

Ryan nodded, before realising that the CIA agent on the line couldn't see him on the other end of the phone. "I understand," he said.

"Excellent," Logan continued. "You want large bills. Get large bills. Put the bills into a shoe box and tape all around the box. On the box, write your name and address and put your signature on it. Now I'm going to give you a locker number, that's the number of the evidence locker. Do you have a pen?"

"Yes," Ryan fumbled to find a pen amongst the pile of clutter on the dining room table.

"Good. The number is 256." Logan repeated the number, emphasising each digit. "2. 5. 6. That's the evidence locker number. Write that number on the box along with your name, address and signature."

"Ok," Ryan said, scribbling the number down on the envelope of an unopened electricity bill.

"So, to recap, you withdraw 50K from the bank in cash, do not alert them or you could be in serious danger. Put the cash in a box and tape the box shut. Write your name, address and signature on the box. Write the number 256 on the box. Got that?"

"Got it," Ryan answered hesitantly. His mind raced with fears of his hard-earned money falling into the wrong hands. He couldn't shake off his doubts and worries, but he also knew he had no other choice but to go through with this risky transaction.

"Excellent. You need to act fast, Ryan. Time is of the essence. The sooner we can secure your money, the better our chances of catching these criminals red-handed," Logan explained, urgency dripping from every word.

"Understood," Ryan said, steeling himself for the task ahead. "When and where do I need to meet your agent?"

"Go to the bank and withdraw the funds first. Once you have the money, call me back, and I will provide you with the details of the meeting point," Logan instructed.

"Okay," Ryan agreed, feeling the weight of responsibility on his shoulders. "I'll head to the bank right away."

"Good luck, Ryan. Remember, don't alert the staff. We're here to help you through this. Call me as soon as you have the money," Logan reminded him before hanging up.

The phone clicked as the line went dead. As Ryan stood there, phone still in hand, he couldn't shake the uneasy feeling that had settled in his chest. But with so much at stake, he knew he had to act quickly. Taking a deep breath, he grabbed his keys, wallet, and coat, and headed out the door, ready to face the unknown.

Chapter 4

"Okay, Ryan," he muttered to himself, climbing into his car and starting the engine. "You've got this." But even as he attempted to reassure himself, his mind was a whirlwind of doubt and confusion.

As he drove towards the bank, Ryan's thoughts were consumed by the events that had just unfolded. The smooth transitions between Amy, Nate, and Logan had been nothing short of impressive. But as he replayed the conversation in his head, he couldn't escape the nagging feeling that something was off.

Ryan's hands tightened on the steering wheel as he navigated through the early morning traffic. The streets were still quiet, with only a few cars and pedestrians out and about. But Ryan's mind was anything but calm.

He couldn't shake off his uneasiness about the whole situation. The smooth transitions between Amazon, the FTC, and the CIA had been smooth, impressive. But something about it felt off. It all seemed too convenient, too perfect.

"Maybe they're just really good at their jobs," he reasoned, gripping the steering wheel tighter. "Or maybe I'm just being paranoid."

Ryan glanced at the rearview mirror, half expecting to see a black sedan tailing him. But there was only the usual traffic, moving along obliviously.

As he pulled into the bank's parking lot, Ryan took a deep breath, steeling himself for what was to come. He grabbed his wallet and got out of the car, making sure to lock it behind him.

As he stood in line, his mind wandered back to Logan's words: "Time is of the essence."

"Next," the teller called, snapping Ryan back to reality. Ryan forced himself to keep a calm demeanor as he approached.

"Hi there," he greeted her with a smile that didn't quite reach his eyes. "I need to withdraw 50 thousand dollars from my account."

"Are you sure you want to withdraw such a large amount?" the teller asked, her eyebrows raised with concern.

"Yes," Ryan replied, his voice wavering. He handed over his driver's license as identification.

As she processed his request, Ryan couldn't help but feel like all eyes were on him. He tried to appear nonchalant as he looked around nervously.

"Please wait here while I get the cash for you," she said, retreating to the vault.

Ryan's palms were slick with sweat, and his eyes darted around the bank, searching for any signs of danger. Every second felt like an eternity.

Finally, the teller returned with a stack of $100 bills. She broke the seal on each rack and dropped them into the counting machine, putting $10,000 in each of 5 envelopes.

"Please sign here, Mr Anderson," the teller said.

Ryan reached for the nearby pen on the countertop and signed the form before slipping it back to the Teller, who swapped the form for the cash.

"Thank you," Ryan stammered, taking the notes and putting them into one of the plastic bags. The weight of it was both exhilarating and terrifying. He rolled the bag up and put it into the other plastic bag so that he wasn't just carrying a bag of loose notes. If someone saw him on the street, they wouldn't know he was carrying so much money. He'd just look like a regular guy carrying some groceries.

As Ryan walked out of the bank, he couldn't help but feel like he was being watched. He quickened his pace, constantly looking over his shoulder to make sure he wasn't being followed.

He reached his car and unlocked it, throwing the bags onto the passenger seat. His hands were shaking as he started the car and drove off.

Even though he had the money in his possession now, Ryan couldn't shake off the feeling of unease. He knew he should be grateful for Logan's help, but something just didn't feel right about the whole situation.

***

As he drove home, Ryan's mind was racing with all sorts of scenarios and possibilities. What if Logan had set him up? What if this was all a trap? What if this was just another part of some elaborate plan?

But then again, what other choice did he have? If he didn't go along with Logan's plan, Ryan would surely end up in prison. And with no evidence or alibi to prove his innocence, it wouldn't take long for him to be convicted.

Ryan pulled into his driveway and sat in his car for a few minutes, trying to calm himself down. He needed to think rationally and come up with a plan.

With a deep breath, Ryan got out of the car and grabbed the bag of money. He quickly made his way inside and locked the door behind him.

He headed straight to his home office and emptied the contents of the bag onto his desk. The sight of so much cash made him feel both elated and nervous.

Ryan's head was spinning with questions and concerns. He grabbed a shoe box from the garage, unsure if all of the cash would fit. Miraculously, at least it seemed so to Ryan, there was plenty of space in the box for the cash. He grabbed the tape from the dining room table, still there from wrapping presents. He needed to get a cleaner. Ryan wrapped up the box in as more tape than he thought would be needed. Enough is just enough, too much is enough, he thought. He picked up an envelope from and wrote his details on it. He checked the number he'd written down. 256. He wrote that under his name and address then signed the envelope and taped that onto the box.

Ryan needed to talk to Logan. He pulled out his phone and dialled the last caller, Logan picked up on the first ring. "Logan," the voice said with an air of authority.

"I've got the money," he gasped, barely able to contain his anxiety. "What do I do now?"

"Good work, Ryan," Logan replied coolly, his voice a stark contrast to Ryan's panicked tone. "Now, listen carefully. This is where everything hangs in the balance."

"Ok," Ryan said, holding the phone closer to his ear.

"We have an undercover agent nearby to collect the box from you. It's crucial that we keep this low-key, Ryan," Logan explained, his tone firm yet persuasive.

"Okay," Ryan said hesitantly, his mind racing with questions, but he swallowed his doubts and focused on the task at hand.

"Meet our agent in 15 minutes. That's a CIA 15 minutes, which is 15 minutes. Not 14, not 16. 15. 15 minutes. Meet him at the park on the corner of 5th and Elm," Logan instructed. "He'll be sitting on a bench, wearing a red baseball cap and a Stanford sweatshirt. Hand him the shoe box and walk away. Don't speak to him, don't make eye contact."

"Got it," Ryan said, his heart pounding as he started the car and headed for the park.

As he approached the park, Ryan spotted the man in the red cap. He took a deep breath, trying to calm his nerves. He parked the car, grabbed the shoe box, and made his way over.

But just as he was about to hand over the box, a nagging doubt crept into his mind. What if this wasn't the undercover agent? What if he was making a terrible mistake?

"Logan," Ryan whispered into the phone, his voice wavering. "How do I know this is really your guy?"

"Is he wearing a red baseball cap and a Stanford sweatshirt?"

"Yes."

"Is there anyone else in the park wearing a red baseball cap and a Stanford sweatshirt?"

"No."

"Then trust me, Ryan," Logan's voice came through the line, steady and reassuring. "Everything's going according to plan. Once the CIA has the box, you are safe. Your money will be safe in the evidence locker, we'll get the check overnighted to you. I have it already printed and ready for the courier as soon as the box is passed to our Agent."

Ryan handed over the shoe box, his gut churning with a mix of fear and anticipation. As he walked away, he couldn't help but wonder if he'd made the right decision – or if he'd just walked straight into a trap.

Ryan's heart hammered in his chest as he watched the man in the red baseball cap stroll away with the shoe box tucked under his arm. He could feel the weight of the phone in his hand, the faint echo of Logan's final words still resonating in his ears.

"Everything's going according to plan," he repeated to himself, trying to swallow the lump of doubt lodged in his throat.

The park was bustling with activity – kids squealing on the playground, joggers huffing past, and couples canoodling on benches. But amidst all the laughter and life, Ryan couldn't shake the sense that something was off.

"Is it really?" he muttered under his breath, staring at the retreating figure in the distance. "Or have I just been played?"

He clenched his fists, frustration and fear mingling together in a potent cocktail. The voice inside his head grew louder, screaming for him to chase after the man and retrieve his money before it was too late.

"Damn it!" Ryan hissed, taking a few hesitant steps forward.

"Hey, mister, you dropped this," a young boy said, tapping Ryan on the shoulder and holding out a crumpled dollar bill.

"Thanks, kid," Ryan replied absentmindedly, pocketing the money. As he did so, the boy's innocent gaze seemed to pierce deep into his soul, making him question his actions even more.

"Is everything okay?" the child asked, his brow furrowed with concern.

"Sure," Ryan forced a smile onto his face, though it felt like a mask over his mounting dread. "Just... a little lost."

"Maybe you should call someone for help," the boy suggested. "My mom always says it's better to ask for help than to keep worrying by yourself."

"Maybe I should," Ryan considered. With a heavy sigh, he turned back to the phone in his hand.

"Logan, are you still there?" he asked hesitantly, his voice barely audible over the cacophony of the park. No response. "Logan?" He tried again, louder this time.

"Ryan," Logan's voice suddenly crackled to life, the sound both reassuring and unsettling at once. "I told you not to worry. We're handling everything."

"Are you sure?" Ryan demanded, his desperation starting to show. "Because I can't shake this feeling that I've made a huge mistake."

"Relax," Logan commanded, his tone sharp but confident. "You did what you needed to do. You're safe now. We'll take care of the rest. No charges filed. Not against you anyway," Logan smirked.

"Okay," Ryan mumbled, uncertainty gnawing at him as he hung up the call. He glanced back at the path the man in the red cap had taken, wondering if he'd ever see his money again – or if he'd just handed it over to a group of cunning strangers with no intention of protecting him or his assets.

"Hey, kid," he called out to the boy who'd returned his dollar. "Thanks for the advice."

"Anytime, mister!" the child beamed, running off to join his friends.

As Ryan watched him go, he couldn't help but feel a pang of envy for the innocence and trust the boy still possessed. He only hoped that he hadn't just gambled away everything he held dear on a single, terrifying roll of the dice.

Chapter 5

The sound of the phone disconnecting left a deafening silence in the room. Logan lowered the phone and locked eyes with Nate and Amy, who had been holding their breaths throughout the call.

"Damn, Logan, you really pulled it off," Nate exclaimed, clapping him on the shoulder. The tension melted away, replaced by an air of anticipation and excitement.

"Couldn't have done it without your guidance, boss," Logan replied, a grin spreading across his bearded face. "Ryan swallowed our story hook, line, and sinker."

Amy stepped forward, her red hair shimmering like fire under the dim light. "Seriously, that was incredible." She raised her hand for a high-five, which Logan eagerly met. "You played Ryan like a fiddle."

"Thanks, Amy. I've gotta say, it was fun playing the part," Logan admitted, rubbing the back of his neck. He couldn't help but feel a sense of pride at having successfully contributed to this crucial step in their plan. It was all coming together now.

"Alright, team," Nate said, clapping his hands together. "Time to finish this. Once we get that shoebox from Ryan, it's game over."

Amy agreed. "We're one step closer to getting Debbie her money back."

"Indeed," Logan added. "And putting that smooth-talking snake in his place."

As Nate prepared to leave, Logan felt a surge of adrenaline coursing through his veins. The thrill of the con, the intricate web of deceit they'd weaved – it had all come down to this final, pivotal moment. And he knew, without a doubt, that they were more than ready for it.

Logan leaned against the kitchen table, a smug grin playing on his lips. "I gotta say, I never thought I'd enjoy this Social Engineering gig as much as I did. Acting the part, getting inside Ryan's head – it was like a game of chess."

"Except with higher stakes," Amy added, her green eyes sparkling with excitement.

"Exactly," Logan agreed, crossing his arms over his chest. "But we've got him right where we want him now. Thanks to you two, of course."

Nate nodded, acknowledging the compliment. "We make one hell of a team, don't we?"

"Absolutely," Amy chimed in, beaming at both men.

"Alright," Nate said, pushing himself off the counter and heading towards the hallway. "Time for me to get ready for the final act." In mere minutes, he emerged dressed in jeans, a Stanford sweatshirt, and a red baseball cap – the expected disguise for the afternoon rendezvous.

"Looking good, Nate," Logan said, giving him a thumbs-up. "You'll blend right in."

"Thanks, man," Nate replied, adjusting the cap on his head. Amy approached him, wrapping her arms around his waist.

"Good luck, Hon," she whispered, pressing a quick kiss to his cheek. "Make sure everything goes smoothly, okay?"

"Will do Sweet," Nate promised, returning her embrace before gently pulling away. "I'll see you both back here soon, with the money in hand."

"Can't wait," Logan grinned. "Knock 'em dead, Nate."

"Or rather, don't," Amy teased, winking at her husband. "Just bring us that shoebox."

"Count on it," Nate said, his voice filled with determination. As he opened the front door, he took a deep breath, steeling himself for the task ahead. It was up to him now – the success of their plan rested on his shoulders. And he wouldn't let anyone down.

"Be careful," Amy called after him as he stepped outside.

"Always am," Nate replied, flashing her a confident smile before closing the door behind him.

Inside the house, Logan and Amy exchanged glances filled with anticipation and concern. They knew the risks involved in this last step, but they also had full faith in Nate's abilities. They had come so far, and now it was all down to their charismatic leader.

***

Nate's heart raced as he walked down the sidewalk, the sun casting elongated shadows in front of him. The bustling park loomed ahead, filled with people enjoying the clear day. He couldn't help but feel the weight of their mission on his shoulders.

"Remember," Amy's voice echoed in his head, "we're counting on you."

"Piece of cake," Nate mumbled under his breath, trying to convince himself more than anyone else. As he neared the park bench where he was supposed to meet Ryan, his senses heightened. He could hear the laughter of children playing nearby, smell the aroma of food from a street vendor, and feel the damp grass beneath his feet. But above it all, he felt the sharp edge of danger lurking just beneath the surface.

"Hey," Logan's voice crackled in his earpiece, "You good?"

"Yup, just peachy," Nate replied, forcing a smile onto his face as he scanned the area for any sign of trouble. His mind raced with thoughts of what could go wrong – an ambush, a double-cross, or worse.

"Relax, man. You got this," Logan reassured him, attempting to alleviate some of the tension.

"Thanks, Logan." Nate took a deep breath, trying to steady his nerves. The thought of failure gnawed at him – if they didn't get the shoebox, everything they had worked for would be for naught.

"Focus, Nate," he whispered to himself as he sat on the designated park bench. He knew that the chances of Ryan getting violent were slim, especially in such a public place, but the nagging fear remained. What if Ryan sensed something was off? What if he had brought backup?

"Clock's ticking," Logan reminded him, his voice tense.

"Got it," Nate replied. He glanced around one last time before settling his gaze on the entrance to the park, waiting for Ryan to appear.

He took a moment to appreciate the beauty of the day – the sun shining brightly in the cloudless sky, casting a warm glow on the world around him. It was almost enough to make him forget the danger that lurked just out of sight.

"Here he comes," Nate whispered as he spotted Ryan approaching, looking nervous and checking over his shoulder. "Showtime."

"Good luck, brother," Logan said, his voice filled with both concern and encouragement.

"Thanks," Nate replied, steeling himself for the crucial moment. He knew that his life, along with the lives of Amy and Logan, hung in the balance. But they were a team, and together, they would see this through to the end – no matter what it took.

A crisp autumn breeze rustled through the golden leaves above as Nate parked the car a block away from the park. He took a deep breath, feeling the chill in the air that matched the tingling of nerves within him. With each step towards the park, he tried to shake off his anxiety and focus on the mission at hand.

"Almost there," he whispered to himself.

As he arrived at the park bench, Nate casually checked his surroundings – families picnicking on the grass, a couple walking their dog, and children laughing as they played on the swings. Such normalcy seemed surreal amidst the high-stakes operation he was about to execute.

"Remember, stay calm and act natural," Amy's voice echoed in his memory, her words offering a sense of comfort.

Nate sat down and glanced at his watch, noting that he was two minutes early. The anticipation gnawed at his insides, but he couldn't let it show. He had to trust in his own abilities and in the team that had his back.

"Hey, Nate," Logan's voice crackled in his earpiece, "You good?"

"Little nervous, but I'll manage," Nate admitted, keeping his eyes on the park entrance.

"Ryan won't suspect a thing. You've got this," Logan reassured him.

"Thanks," Nate replied, taking a deep breath and running through the plan one last time in his head. He knew that if any part went wrong, everything they'd worked for would be lost – and the danger wasn't just financial.

"Focus, Nate," he thought as the seconds ticked by. Each passing moment felt like an eternity, heightening his awareness of his surroundings. He reminded himself that it was daylight and the risk of violence was low, yet he couldn't help but imagine worst-case scenarios.

"Two minutes," Logan reminded him, his voice tense but steady.

"Got it," Nate responded, trying to keep his tone even. He scanned the park once more, appreciating the sunlight filtering through the trees and casting dappled shadows on the ground. The beauty of the day seemed at odds with the dark undercurrents of their operation.

"Here's hoping this goes smoothly," he thought, clenching his hands in anticipation. As the final moments approached, he knew that everything was riding on this one crucial exchange – and he couldn't afford to let doubt or fear get in the way.

"Good luck, brother" Logan said, his voice filled with both concern and encouragement.

"Thanks," Nate replied, steeling himself for the critical moment. He knew that his life, along with the lives of Amy and Logan, hung in the balance. But they were a team, and together, they would see this through to the end – no matter what it took.

A flash of short dark hair caught Nate's eye, and his heartbeat quickened. Ryan Anderson appeared at the edge of the park, his piercing blue eyes darting around nervously as he checked over his shoulder. Nate could see that Ryan's charm had temporarily deserted him – it seemed that even master manipulators could feel the pressure.

"Showtime," Nate murmured under his breath, watching intently as Ryan began to make his way towards him.

"Stay sharp, Nate. He's on edge," Amy's voice sounded in his earpiece, a reminder that she and Logan were with him every step of the way.

"Copy that," he replied, focusing on steadying his breathing and maintaining a casual appearance.

As Ryan walked closer, Nate could see the sheen of sweat on his forehead, betraying the tension beneath his carefully constructed facade. This was the moment they'd all been working towards, and Nate knew that one misstep could jeopardize everything.

"Keep calm. Trust the plan," he silently coached himself, drawing on his military background for mental resilience.

Ryan neared the bench, moving slower than before as if he was trying to appear inconspicuous. Nate pretended not to notice him, taking out his phone and scrolling through it as if he were just another park-goer enjoying the day.

"Here we go," Nate thought, his heart racing.

With practiced nonchalance, Ryan extended his arm as he passed by, handing the shoebox to Nate without breaking stride or making eye contact. In an instant, the exchange was made, and Nate felt the weight of the box in his hands.

"Got it," Nate whispered into his earpiece, knowing the importance of what he now held. The fate of their mission rested within this small cardboard container, and he couldn't help but feel a thrill of excitement mixed with anxiety.

"Good job, now get out of there," Logan instructed, his voice steady and confident.

"Will do," Nate replied, standing up and walking in the opposite direction from Ryan. The adrenaline coursed through his veins as he took each step, his mind racing with thoughts of what would happen next – had they truly succeeded, or was this just another twist in their intricate game? One thing was for certain: they were about to find out.

The sun glinted off the golden leaves above as Nate stood, feeling the weight of the shoebox in his hands. He began to walk away, each step crisp and purposeful, like a predator stalking its prey. His heart pounded in his chest, but outwardly he showed no signs of distress, his military training coming to the fore.

"Everything good?" Amy's voice buzzed in his ear.

"Got the box," Nate replied, voice low and steady. "Heading back now."

"Be careful," she warned, her concern for him seeping through the line.

"Always am." Nate allowed himself a small smile, his love for Amy and her unwavering support pushing him onward.

As Nate continued to walk briskly, he wondered what was inside the shoebox. Did it actually contain the money they were after, or had Ryan uncovered their ruse? The uncertainty gnawed at him, sending tendrils of doubt into his mind.

Nate focused on putting one foot in front of the other. His mind raced with possibilities, each step bringing him closer to the truth. But there was still that nagging fear – what if they'd failed? What if they'd pushed too hard and spooked Ryan into backing out? The thought sent a chill down his spine, but he shook it off, reminding himself that they'd come this far and wouldn't give up without a fight.

"Almost there," Nate said into his earpiece, spotting the car in the distance. He clutched the shoebox tighter, as if it were a lifeline. If it contained the money, they'd be one step closer to justice for Debbie. If not... well, they'd cross that bridge when they came to it.

"Stay sharp," Amy warned. "You never know what could happen."

"I know," Nate replied, his eyes scanning the area for any signs of danger. His military instincts were on high alert, ready for action at a moment's notice. But as he neared the car, no threats emerged, and he allowed himself a small sigh of relief.

"Almost home free," Nate thought, his mind racing with anticipation. Soon, they would have their answer – had they succeeded, or had Ryan outsmarted them all? The moment of truth loomed ever closer, and Nate couldn't help but feel a thrill of exhilaration mixed with apprehension.

"See you soon," Amy's voice said softly in his ear.

"Can't wait," Nate replied, his voice filled with determination. With the shoebox in hand, he strode purposefully toward the car, knowing that victory or defeat lay just moments away.

***

Nate's heart pounded in his chest as he eased the car into the driveway, the shoebox cradled in his lap. He could feel the weight of it, but whether it was filled with money or something else altogether remained to be seen. He killed the engine and glanced up at the house, noticing Amy and Logan waiting expectantly by the front door.

"Here goes nothing," Nate muttered, stepping out of the car. He couldn't help but tighten his grip on the box as he approached them, his nerves frayed from the tension.

"Is that it?" Logan asked, his voice a mix of excitement and concern.

"Only one way to find out," Nate replied, his eyes locked on the box. They all stepped inside, the door shutting behind them with an ominous click.

"Let's get to it," Amy said, her voice steady despite the anticipation coursing through her. She retrieved a pair of scissors from a nearby drawer and carefully sliced through the tape sealing the box.

"Cross your fingers, guys," Nate thought, his gaze never leaving the shoebox. It felt like an eternity passed before Amy finally finished cutting all of the tape and opened the lid.

As the shoebox's contents were revealed, a collective sigh of relief filled the room. Stacked neatly inside were rows of crisp $100 bills – $50,000 worth, just as they'd hoped.

"Thank God," Logan breathed, his face breaking into a wide grin. "We actually pulled it off."

"Looks that way," Nate agreed, his own smile slowly emerging. The adrenaline began to fade, replaced by a sense of accomplishment and satisfaction.

Amy couldn't suppress a laugh, her eyes shining with unshed tears of joy. "We did it. We really did it." She looked at Nate and Logan, her partners in this risky endeavor. "We got Debbie's money back."

"Damn right we did," Logan said, clapping Nate on the back. "Couldn't have done it without you, man."

"Or you," Nate replied, returning the gesture. He glanced at Amy, his eyes filled with gratitude and love. "Or you, my brilliant wife."

"Team effort," Amy agreed, her smile never wavering.

For a moment, they simply stood there, basking in the knowledge that their plan had succeeded. The risks they'd taken, the lives they'd put on the line – it had all been worth it. They had outsmarted Ryan and reclaimed what was rightfully Debbie's, and in doing so, they had proven once again that justice could prevail against even the most difficult odds.

"Let's celebrate," Logan suggested, his voice brimming with enthusiasm. "We earned it."

"Sounds like a plan," Nate agreed, his mind already turning to how this victory would change Debbie's life for the better. "But first, let's make sure this money gets to where it belongs."

Nate watched as the sunlight danced across the stacks of hundred-dollar bills, casting a warm golden glow over the room. The air was thick with the weight of relief and triumph, as if the very atmosphere itself knew what they had just achieved.

"Mission accomplished." Logan's words were laced with pride, and he exhaled deeply, clearly releasing tension that had been building throughout their daring escapade.

"Damn right," Amy chimed in, her eyes sparkling with excitement. "It feels so good to know we got Debbie's money back from that scumbag."

"Here's to teamwork," Nate said, raising an imaginary glass in a toast, a grin spreading across his face. "We couldn't have done it without each other."

"Cheers to that," Amy agreed, laughing as she mimicked Nate's gesture. Logan joined in, and the three of them shared a moment of light-hearted camaraderie.

As the laughter died down, Nate found himself reflecting on the events that led them here. The planning, the risks, and the execution – all driven by their determination to see justice served. It was funny, in a way, how such a serious mission could bring out the humor and creativity in each of them. But perhaps that was what made it work. They were a team, bound together by trust and determination.

"Debbie deserves this," Nate mused aloud, his thoughts returning to the woman at the heart of it all. "She's been through so much, and now she can finally start rebuilding her life."

"Absolutely," Amy agreed, her voice softening as she thought of the grieving widow. "I can't wait to see the look on her face when she sees this."

"Me neither," Logan added, his own grin turning thoughtful. "You know, I've learned a lot from this whole experience. Social engineering isn't just about manipulation and deceit; it's about understanding people, knowing what makes them tick. It's a tool, like any other, and you can use it for good or bad."

"True," Nate nodded, considering Logan's words. "And in this case, we were able to use it for the greater good. That's something to be proud of."

"Definitely," Amy smiled, her gaze lingering on the shoebox full of cash. "But let's not forget that we still have one more thing left to do."

"Right," Nate agreed, his determination returning. "Let's get this money to Debbie, and then we can celebrate our victory properly."

"Agreed," said Logan, clapping Nate on the shoulder. "But after all this, I better get an invite to the party."

"Of course," Nate grinned back. "You're part of the team now, after all."

Chapter 6

The aroma of freshly brewed coffee enveloped the small table where Nate, Amy, Logan, and Debbie sat, providing a soothing backdrop to the tension simmering in the air.

"Alright, let's make sure it's all here," Nate said, his eyes scanning the stacks of cash as he began counting them with practiced precision. His military background had taught him the value of thoroughness, and he knew that leaving nothing to chance was crucial for Debbie's peace of mind.

Amy noticed Debbie's hands trembling in her lap. She reached over and placed a reassuring hand on Debbie's shoulder, feeling the tension beneath the fabric of her blouse. "It's going to be okay," she whispered, her own experiences with loss and betrayal lending empathy to her words.

"Thank you," Debbie murmured, her voice barely audible.

Nate finally looked up from the stacks of bills, locking eyes with Debbie. "Every single dollar is accounted for."

Debbie exhaled shakily, tears pooling at the corners of her eyes as the weight of her ordeal began to lift. "I can't thank you enough," she whispered, the gratitude etched into every line of her face.

"Think nothing of it," Nate replied, his dark eyes warm as he regarded her. "This is what we do - help those who need it most."

"Besides," Amy chimed in, her red hair catching the sunlight streaming through the coffee shop window. "You deserve a fresh start."

As they wrapped up their conversation, Nate felt a sense of fulfillment and purpose coursing through him. He knew that, together with Amy and Logan, they had made a real difference in Debbie's life - and there were countless others out there who needed their unique blend of skills and determination.

"Let's drink to that," Logan suggested, raising his cup of coffee in a toast.

"Here's to new beginnings," Amy added, clinking her cup against Debbie's.

"New beginnings," Debbie echoed, a hint of a smile breaking through her tears as she joined them in the simple yet meaningful gesture.

The comforting weight of Amy's hand on Debbie's shoulder anchored her to the present, providing solace amidst the whirlwind of emotions swirling within her. "How can I ever thank you all enough?" she asked, her voice trembling with gratitude.

"Debbie," Nate began, his eyes softening as he met her gaze, "we promised we'd help you, and we meant it. You don't owe us anything."

"Exactly," Logan chimed in, a slight smirk playing at the corners of his mouth. "We couldn't just let some slick scammer get away with taking advantage of a nice lady like yourself, now could we?"

Debbie smiled through her tears, touched by their unwavering dedication. She knew that trusting them had been a leap of faith, but they had proven themselves to be true allies in her time of need.

"Still," she insisted, wiping her damp cheeks, "I can't express how grateful I am. You three have given me hope when I thought I had lost everything."

Logan raised an eyebrow, his laid-back demeanor momentarily replaced by a look of genuine concern. He glanced at Nate and Amy for reassurance before responding. "Debbie, sometimes life throws a curveball our way, but there are always people willing to help. We've got your back, no matter what."

"Thank you," Debbie whispered, feeling the knot in her chest slowly unravel as she accepted the truth in Logan's words. She allowed herself a moment to bask in the warmth of their support, recognizing that she was not alone in her struggles.

In the midst of the bustling coffee shop, Nate exchanged a knowing glance with Amy and Logan. Each of them understood the importance of using their unique skills for good, helping those who had been wronged by people who preyed on the vulnerable.

As Debbie collected her thoughts, she looked at her new friends with renewed appreciation. She knew that their paths had crossed for a reason, and she was grateful for the opportunity to move forward with a newfound sense of hope.

"Here's to new beginnings," she declared, raising her cup of coffee in a toast.

"New beginnings," Nate, Amy, and Logan echoed, clinking their cups together in a symbolic gesture of triumph and solidarity.

Nate leaned in toward Debbie, his eyes reflecting the sincerity within. "Justice has been served. That scammer won't be able to hurt you or anyone else again." He paused for a beat, allowing his words to sink in. "You can move forward now, with hope and trust in others."

Debbie's gaze lingered on Nate's face, searching for any trace of doubt or deception. But all she saw was genuine concern and conviction. She turned her attention to Amy and Logan, who both nodded in agreement. A surge of relief washed over her as it became clear that these three people had truly dedicated themselves to helping her overcome her ordeal.

"Thank you," she whispered, her voice barely audible amidst the gentle hum of the coffee shop's background conversations. Her eyes welled up with tears as she let the full weight of their actions settle upon her heart. She felt a renewed sense of hope, realizing that there were still good people in this world – people who went out of their way to help those in need. It was a stark contrast to the darkness she'd experienced at the hands of the scammer.

"Hey," Logan said softly, breaking the silence. "We're just doing what's right. You deserve better than what happened to you."

Amy reached across the table, gently squeezing Debbie's hand. "That's right. You've got friends here who'll always have your back."

The comforting touch and the kindness in Amy's eyes finally broke through Debbie's emotional defenses. The tears spilled over, streaming down her cheeks as she tried to blink them away. She managed a watery smile, knowing that despite the pain of her past, she could look forward to a brighter future thanks to the unwavering dedication of Nate, Amy, and Logan.

"You guys... I don't know how I can ever repay you for everything you've done," she choked out between sobs.

"Your happiness and safety are all the payment we need," Nate assured her, his voice firm yet gentle. "Just remember, you're not alone in this world. There are people who care."

As she wiped away her tears, Debbie looked at each of them in turn, feeling a newfound strength building within her. With friends like these by her side, she could face whatever challenges life had in store for her. And with that thought, she knew she could finally begin to heal.

Debbie watched as the steam from their coffee cups danced and intertwined in the air, much like the intricate web of lies they had untangled together. Her heart swelled with gratitude for these three strangers who had become her allies.

"Let's celebrate," Amy declared, raising her coffee cup high. "To justice... to new friendships... and to moving forward."

Debbie looked into the deep brown of her own coffee, momentarily lost in the swirling patterns. This was a turning point, she realized. A chance to leave the darkness of the past behind and embrace the unknown with courage.

"Here's to all the good people out there," Nate added, lifting his cup with a warm smile.

"Especially those who never give up on helping others," Logan chimed in.

Their words hung in the air, as if carried by the aroma of roasted coffee beans. And in that moment, Debbie found herself part of something greater than herself – a bond forged in the pursuit of justice.

As their cups came together in a triumphant clink, Debbie couldn't help but smile through her tears. For the first time in months, she felt lightness return to her heart. The burden of her grief, her fear, and her mistrust began to lift ever so slightly.

"Thank you," she whispered, her voice barely audible over the din of the coffee shop. "For everything."

"Anytime, Debbie," Amy replied, her green eyes sparkling with determination. "We're here for you."

"Remember," Nate said, leaning in closer, "you're not alone. We'll always be just a phone call away."

"Or a text message," Logan added with a grin. "I mean, it is the twenty-first century."

Debbie chuckled at his attempt at humor, feeling the ice around her heart begin to thaw. It was true – she wasn't alone anymore. In this cozy coffee shop, surrounded by the comforting scents and sounds of life moving forward, she had found a new family.

***

The sun cast a warm, golden glow on the trio as they exited the coffee shop. Nate took a deep breath, inhaling the crisp autumn air, and felt a surge of satisfaction wash over him. In moments like these, he knew that the path he'd chosen – helping those who had been wronged – was exactly where he was meant to be.

"Guys," Logan began, his voice serious despite the slight smirk tugging at the corner of his mouth, "we've got something special here. I mean, we're taking down scammers and giving people back their hope. It's not every day you get to do that."

Amy nodded in agreement, her eyes sparkling with conviction. "We've been given these skills for a reason. We can't just sit back and do nothing when we know we can make a difference."

Nate looked at the determined faces of his wife and friend and felt a renewed sense of purpose. They were right; they had a unique opportunity to help people, to fight against injustice. He imagined the countless others like Debbie out there, struggling to find hope in the face of deceit and betrayal.

"Let's keep going," Nate said decisively, locking eyes with Amy and Logan. "Let's use our abilities to bring more justice to this world. There are people out there who need us – people whose lives have been shattered by scams and fraud."

"Count me in," Logan replied without hesitation, his grin widening. "I'm always up for a good fight."

"Me too," Amy chimed in softly, her hand reaching out to grip Nate's tightly. "Together, we'll make a real impact."

As they walked away from the coffee shop, Nate mulled over their next move. In his mind, he saw a mental list forming, filled with names and faces of those who had been wronged. The weight of responsibility settled on his shoulders, but the fire in his heart burned brighter, fueled by the knowledge that they were making a difference.

"Every life we touch," he thought, "is one less person left to suffer alone."

Chapter 7

The dim glow of computer screens and a solitary desk lamp cast eerie shadows on the walls of the makeshift office. Nate and Amy, the husband and wife duo responsible for Debbie Thompson's newfound sense of justice, sat in their matching swivel chairs, their faces illuminated by the soft light. Surrounded by stacks of documents, they let out simultaneous sighs, leaning back after their latest successful mission.

"Another one for the books," Nate muttered, rubbing his tired eyes. The adrenaline from earlier had worn off, replaced by exhaustion. He glanced at Amy, her red hair loose around her shoulders, her hazel eyes reflecting the computer screen before her. But he could see the pride and satisfaction in them as well.

Amy nodded, running her fingers through her hair. "It feels good to help people like Debbie. To know we've made a difference in her life." Her voice was soft but firm, the words carrying weight.

For a moment, they sat in silence, allowing the gravity of what they had accomplished to sink in. It wasn't just about the money they'd recovered; it was about giving Debbie the security and peace of mind she desperately needed after her husband's passing. Nate felt a pang of empathy, remembering the loss he'd experienced in his own life. It fueled his determination to help others, like Debbie, who were vulnerable and in need.

"Hey," Amy said suddenly, breaking the silence. She reached out and squeezed Nate's hand, her eyes meeting his with sincerity. "We're doing important work here, Nate. You know that, right?"

Nate felt a surge of warmth at Amy's touch, and he squeezed her hand in return. "I do," he replied, his voice filled with conviction. "It's why we started this business, to use our skills for something meaningful."

Amy smiled, her eyes sparkling. "I just wanted to make sure you still believed in it after all these years."

Nate chuckled. "You know me too well," he said, playfully rolling his eyes.

"But seriously," Amy continued, her expression turning serious again. "Do you ever think about what we'd be doing if we didn't have this business? How our lives would be different?"

Nate furrowed his brow, considering her question. He had never really thought about it before. "I suppose I would still be working at that accounting firm, crunching numbers all day," he said with a shudder.

"And I would probably still be stuck in a dead-end job at that call center," Amy added with a smirk.

They both let out a laugh, the tension easing from the conversation.

"I'm glad we took the leap and started this together," Nate said sincerely.

"Me too," Amy agreed, leaning over to give him a kiss on the cheek.

As they sat back in their chairs, Nate felt grateful for everything they had achieved together. They may not have flashy jobs or high-paying salaries like their friends from college, but they were making a difference in people's lives and that was more fulfilling than any amount of money could ever be.

They shared a knowing look, reflecting on the many missions they'd carried out together. They'd come a long way since their first case, learning from each other and growing stronger as a unit. And as they sat there, amidst the chaos of their office, Nate and Amy knew they were ready to face whatever challenges awaited them.

"Here's to us," Nate said, lifting an imaginary toast in the air.

"Here's to us," Amy echoed, her smile radiant. And together, they held onto that moment of triumph, knowing it would fuel them through the next case and beyond.

With their cups raised in celebration, Nate and Amy basked in the knowledge that they were making a difference in the world, one case at a time. As they set their mugs down, the shadows cast by the computer screens seemed to grow stronger, as if urging them forward towards the next challenge.

"Remember the moment when you hacked into the security system?" Nate asked, a hint of excitement coloring his voice. "I was sweating bullets, thinking we'd get caught."

Amy grinned, leaning back in her chair. "Of course, but every second counted. Your distraction was on point, giving me just enough time to find the right access codes." Her fingers tapped an imaginary keyboard as she relived the thrill of cracking the code.

"Ah, yes," Nate said with a chuckle, rubbing his hands together. "The old 'spilled coffee' routine. Works like a charm every time." He mimed dropping a cup and watched as Amy's laughter filled the room.

"Let's not forget your eagle-eyed spotting of the hidden camera," Amy added, pointing to her eyes and then at Nate. "If it weren't for you, we'd have been recorded and exposed."

Nate held up his hands, feigning modesty. "It was nothing, really. Just putting my military training to good use."

In the silence that followed, Nate studied Amy's face, illuminated by the flickering light of the computer screens. He admired the determination etched into her features, the passion that drove her to fight for justice. He knew that without her quick thinking and keen eye for detail, their operation would never have been successful.

"Seriously, though, Amy," he said, his voice heavy with sincerity. "Your instincts and abilities never cease to amaze me. You're the reason we pulled this off so flawlessly."

Amy blushed slightly, unused to the praise. "Thanks, Nate. But you know we're a team. Your skills at reading people and creating opportunities are just as crucial."

He nodded, taking her words to heart. They were two halves of a whole, each bringing unique talents to the table. Together, they formed an unstoppable force in their quest for justice. And as they sat there, basking in their shared triumph, Nate knew that there was nothing they couldn't accomplish.

"Your ability to read people, Nate... it's uncanny," Amy said, her voice filled with admiration. "You can manipulate situations like nobody else I know. This mission would have been a disaster without you."

Nate leaned back in his chair, his dark eyes reflecting the light from the screens. He ran a hand through his hair, relishing the praise but also feeling humbled by it. "Thank you, Amy. But let's not forget the power of teamwork. We couldn't have done this without each other's unique abilities."

Amy nodded, her red curls dancing in the soft light. She reached across the narrow space between them, resting her hand on Nate's forearm. Her touch sent a warm shiver down his spine, reminding him that they were not only partners in crime-fighting, but also in life.

"You're right," she said, her emerald eyes sparkling with determination. "Our partnership is our greatest strength. We balance each other out and push one another to be better. It's what makes us unstoppable."

Nate felt a surge of pride as he looked at Amy, their faces illuminated by the ghostly glow of the screens. They had faced countless challenges together, both personally and professionally, and had come out stronger every time. The trust and respect they shared was a testament to the power of their bond.

The weight of their accomplishments settled upon them, Nate found himself lost in thought, contemplating the intricacies of their partnership. He marveled at how Amy's investigative journalism background meshed so seamlessly with his military training and hacking skills. Each mission they took on was a new adventure, a chance for them to prove that together, they could make a difference in the world.

"Here's to us," Nate said, raising his coffee mug in a toast. "To our unshakable bond and our relentless pursuit of justice."

Amy raised her own mug, clinking it gently against Nate's. "To us," she echoed, her voice filled with conviction. As they took a sip of their lukewarm coffee, Nate couldn't help but smile at the thought of the many more adventures that awaited them.

"This is why we do what we do, Amy," he said softly, his voice barely audible above the whir of the computers. "To make a difference, to help people like Debbie."

Amy, her fingers hovering above the keyboard, looked up from the screen with a nod, her eyes shining with determination.

Nate smiled at the fire in her voice. He knew how deeply she cared about their mission, and it reminded him of just how much they had been through together. As he watched her dive back into her work, he felt a surge of pride, not just for their recent success, but for every time they had fought side by side for what was right.

"Remember that time in Miami?" he asked, grinning at the memory. "When you hacked into that drug lord's bank account and transferred all his money to a charity for orphaned children?"

"Of course I remember," Amy replied, rolling her eyes but smiling nonetheless. "I'll never forget the look on his face when he realized what we'd done. It was priceless." She paused for a moment, her fingers stilling on the keys. "But we can't afford to rest on our laurels, Nate. There are countless more people out there who need our help."

"Right you are," Nate agreed, his expression turning serious once more. "We've got our work cut out for us."

He returned his focus to the documents in front of him, Nate was filled with a renewed sense of purpose. He knew that their fight for justice would never truly be over, but the knowledge that they were making a tangible difference in people's lives made it all worthwhile.

The dim light of the makeshift office flickered, casting a warm glow over the stacks of documents and multiple computer screens. Nate's eyes caught the steam rising from two mugs of coffee that Amy had just prepared for them. He inhaled deeply, taking in the rich aroma that filled the room.

"Here," Amy said, handing him one of the mugs, her green eyes twinkling with excitement. "We definitely earned this."

"Damn right we did." Nate couldn't help but grin as he raised his mug to Amy. "To Debbie, and to giving her the justice she deserved."

"Cheers!" Amy replied, her voice filled with joy as their mugs clinked together.

They took slow sips of the hot liquid, allowing the warmth to spread through their bodies, a sensation that was both comforting and invigorating. As they savored the moment, Nate marveled at the way Amy's red hair seemed to come alive in the dim light, a fiery symbol of determination and strength.

"Y'know, I'm really glad we were able to help Debbie," he said, his voice tinged with emotion. "Seeing her smile again... well, it reminded me of why we do this."

"Me too," agreed Amy, her own eyes shining with unshed tears. "It's moments like these that make all the risks worthwhile."

Nate nodded, setting down his mug and reaching for her hand. His fingers gently squeezed hers, a silent acknowledgment of their shared purpose and passion for justice. "Promise me something, Amy?"

"Anything," she replied, her gaze never leaving his.

"Promise me we'll never stop fighting for those who can't fight for themselves," Nate said, his voice strong and determined. "That no matter how hard it gets or how many obstacles we face, we'll always stand up for what's right."

"I promise," Amy whispered, her voice equally resolute. "And I know you'll do the same."

"Damn right I will," Nate declared, a fierce smile spreading across his face.

As they held each other's gaze, their hands still intertwined, Nate felt a renewed surge of determination course through his veins. Together, they were unstoppable, a force for good in a world that all too often seemed to reward cruelty and greed. And as long as they had each other, nothing would stand in their way.

"Alright then," he said, releasing Amy's hand and leaning back in his chair, his eyes alight with resolve. "Let's get back to work. There are plenty more people out there who need our help."

"Couldn't have said it better myself," Amy agreed

More?

If this book has captured your imagination and left you yearning for more, I am thrilled to share that it is part of a larger series. Each book delves into the lives of the characters and the plotlines that unfold.

To continue the journey, you can find the other books in the series available for download at http://idsfa.co.uk/where you'll find links to all major online publishers

***

CheckMate

https://books2read.com/b/bwQLj9[1]

In the heart of the city, a vulnerable soul is exploited by a powerful tycoon. But when a husband and wife team takes up the fight for justice, they embark on an elaborate and risky mission to extract money from the tycoon and right the wrongs committed.

With their impeccable reputation as high-profile consultants, they cunningly position themselves as experts in the tycoon's interests and values. Orchestrating a meeting that captivates his attention, they unveil an irresistible offer that seems to align perfectly with his ambitions. As the stakes rise, they skillfully tap into his fear of missing out and desire for greatness, gradually escalating the investment with promises of astronomical returns and exclusive perks.

But this elaborate con isn't just about money. The husband and wife team's ultimate goal is to expose the tycoon's exploitation and demand restitution for the victim. With undeniable evidence in their hands, they confront the tycoon, threatening to expose him publicly and unleash legal and reputational consequences.

---

1. https://books2read.com/b/bwQLj9

As the tycoon faces the potential ruin of his empire and confronts his own moral compass, he undergoes a transformation. But can the husband and wife team trust him to fulfill his promises? With every twist and turn, they must stay one step ahead of the tycoon and navigate a treacherous path to justice.

Will the husband and wife team succeed in their mission and bring justice to the victim? Or will their plan crumble, leaving them with regrets and the tycoon unscathed? Discover the truth in this gripping tale of revenge, redemption, and the pursuit of justice.

***

The Great Escape

https://books2read.com/u/bPzqXx[2]

In a world where justice is elusive, Nate and Amy emerge as an unstoppable force against the dark forces of human trafficking. Nate, an ex-military white-hat hacker, and Amy, a fearless investigative journalist, join forces to form a modern-day A-Team.

Their latest mission takes them deep into the heart of a religious commune, where young girls are held captive under the guise of spirituality. With the cult leader using twisted interpretations of the Bible to justify his heinous acts, Nate and Amy must infiltrate the operation and expose the truth.

They gain the trust of the cult leader and unravel the intricate web of his trafficking ring. But as they dig deeper, they discover that this is just the tip of the iceberg, with a larger operation lurking in the shadows.

Armed with intelligence and cunning, Nate and Amy race against time to dismantle the operation and save as many lives as possible. There are no guns in this battle, only the power of their minds and unwavering determination.

---

2. https://books2read.com/u/bPzqXx

This action-packed thriller takes readers on a heart-stopping journey through the depths of human trafficking. With every page, they witness the atrocities and feel the adrenaline-fueled pursuit of justice.

With a gripping climax that will leave readers breathless, this novel is a testament to the resilience of the human spirit and the unwavering fight against injustice. A must-read for those seeking a thrilling and morally charged adventure.

Acknowledgements

You.

First and foremost, I would like to express my heartfelt gratitude for choosing to embark on this journey with me. Your decision to purchase this book means the world to me, and I am truly honored to have you as a reader.

Writing this book has been an incredible labor of love, filled with numerous late nights, countless cups of coffee, and unyielding determination. However, it is your presence here that gives my words purpose and breathes life into the pages.

I humbly ask for a moment of your time to share your thoughts and experiences with this book. If you found solace within its pages, if it made you smile, laugh, or shed a tear, please consider leaving a review. Your feedback is invaluable, not only to me but also to other potential readers who may be searching for their next read.

Your review, whether it be a few heartfelt words or a detailed analysis, has the power to influence others and guide them towards this world I have created. By sharing your thoughts, you are not only supporting my work but also helping to create a community of readers who can connect and engage with one another.

I understand that time is precious, and writing a review may seem like a small task in the grand scheme of things. However, I assure you that your words have the ability to make a significant impact, allowing this book to reach even greater heights and touch the lives of more readers.

Once again, thank you for your trust and for joining me on this adventure. Your support means everything to me, and I am forever grateful.

With deepest appreciation,

- Shane

Don't miss out!

Visit the website below and you can sign up to receive emails whenever Shane Reed publishes a new book. There's no charge and no obligation.

https://books2read.com/r/B-A-LSDAB-GEZZC

BOOKS 2 READ

Connecting independent readers to independent writers.

Also by Shane Reed

A Conning Couple Novel
Checkmate
The Great Escape
The Queen's Gambit
The Sicilian Defense
Fool's Mate
The Conning Couple Books 1-5

www.ingramcontent.com/pod-product-compliance
Lightning Source LLC
Chambersburg PA
CBHW051254160726
47994CB00003B/1166